# No Thoroughfare

Charles Dickens and Wilkie Collins

ESPRIOS DIGITAL PUBLISHING

## THE OVERTURE.

Day of the month and year, November the thirtieth, one thousand eight hundred and thirty-five. London Time by the great clock of Saint Paul's, ten at night. All the lesser London churches strain their metallic throats. Some, flippantly begin before the heavy bell of the great cathedral; some, tardily begin three, four, half a dozen, strokes behind it; all are in sufficiently near accord, to leave a resonance in the air, as if the winged father who devours his children, had made a sounding sweep with his gigantic scythe in flying over the city.

What is this clock lower than most of the rest, and nearer to the ear, that lags so far behind to-night as to strike into the vibration alone? This is the clock of the Hospital for Foundling Children. Time was, when the Foundlings were received without question in a cradle at the gate. Time is, when inquiries are made respecting them, and they are taken as by favour from the mothers who relinquish all natural knowledge of them and claim to them for evermore.

The moon is at the full, and the night is fair with light clouds. The day has been otherwise than fair, for slush and mud, thickened with the droppings of heavy fog, lie black in the streets. The veiled lady who flutters up and down near the postern-gate of the Hospital for Foundling Children has need to be well shod to-night.

She flutters to and fro, avoiding the stand of hackney-coaches, and often pausing in the shadow of the western end of the great quadrangle wall, with her face turned towards the gate. As above her there is the purity of the moonlit sky, and below her there are the defilements of the pavement, so may she, haply, be divided in her mind between two vistas of reflection or experience. As her footprints crossing and recrossing one another have made a labyrinth in the mire, so may her track in life have involved itself in an intricate and unravellable tangle.

The postern-gate of the Hospital for Foundling Children opens, and a young woman comes out. The lady stands aside, observes closely, sees that the gate is quietly closed again from within, and follows the young woman.

Two or three streets have been traversed in silence before she, following close behind the object of her attention, stretches out her hand and touches her. Then the young woman stops and looks round, startled.

"You touched me last night, and, when I turned my head, you would not speak. Why do you follow me like a silent ghost? "

"It was not, " returned the lady, in a low voice, "that I would not speak, but that I could not when I tried. "

"What do you want of me? I have never done you any harm? "

"Never. "

"Do I know you? "

"No. "

"Then what can you want of me? "

"Here are two guineas in this paper. Take my poor little present, and I will tell you. "

Into the young woman's face, which is honest and comely, comes a flush as she replies: "There is neither grown person nor child in all the large establishment that I belong to, who hasn't a good word for Sally. I am Sally. Could I be so well thought of, if I was to be bought? "

"I do not mean to buy you; I mean only to reward you very slightly. "

Sally firmly, but not ungently, closes and puts back the offering hand. "If there is anything I can do for you, ma'am, that I will not do for its own sake, you are much mistaken in me if you think that I will do it for money. What is it you want? "

"You are one of the nurses or attendants at the Hospital; I saw you leave to-night and last night. "

"Yes, I am. I am Sally. "

"There is a pleasant patience in your face which makes me believe that very young children would take readily to you. "

"God bless 'em! So they do. "

The lady lifts her veil, and shows a face no older than the nurse's. A face far more refined and capable than hers, but wild and worn with sorrow.

"I am the miserable mother of a baby lately received under your care. I have a prayer to make to you. "

Instinctively respecting the confidence which has drawn aside the veil, Sally—whose ways are all ways of simplicity and spontaneity—replaces it, and begins to cry.

"You will listen to my prayer? " the lady urges. "You will not be deaf to the agonised entreaty of such a broken suppliant as I am? "

"O dear, dear, dear! " cries Sally. "What shall I say, or can say! Don't talk of prayers. Prayers are to be put up to the Good Father of All, and not to nurses and such. And there! I am only to hold my place for half a year longer, till another young woman can be trained up to it. I am going to be married. I shouldn't have been out last night, and I shouldn't have been out to-night, but that my Dick (he is the young man I am going to be married to) lies ill, and I help his mother and sister to watch him. Don't take on so, don't take on so! "

"O good Sally, dear Sally, " moans the lady, catching at her dress entreatingly. "As you are hopeful, and I am hopeless; as a fair way in life is before you, which can never, never, be before me; as you can aspire to become a respected wife, and as you can aspire to become a proud mother, as you are a living loving woman, and must die; for GOD'S sake hear my distracted petition! "

"Deary, deary, deary ME! " cries Sally, her desperation culminating in the pronoun, "what am I ever to do? And there! See how you turn my own words back upon me. I tell you I am going to be married, on purpose to make it clearer to you that I am going to leave, and therefore couldn't help you if I would, Poor Thing, and you make it seem to my own self as if I was cruel in going to be married and not helping you. It ain't kind. Now, is it kind, Poor Thing? "

"Sally! Hear me, my dear. My entreaty is for no help in the future. It applies to what is past. It is only to be told in two words. "

"There! This is worse and worse, " cries Sally, "supposing that I understand what two words you mean. "

3

"You do understand. What are the names they have given my poor baby? I ask no more than that. I have read of the customs of the place. He has been christened in the chapel, and registered by some surname in the book. He was received last Monday evening. What have they called him? "

Down upon her knees in the foul mud of the by-way into which they have strayed—an empty street without a thoroughfare giving on the dark gardens of the Hospital—the lady would drop in her passionate entreaty, but that Sally prevents her.

"Don't! Don't! You make me feel as if I was setting myself up to be good. Let me look in your pretty face again. Put your two hands in mine. Now, promise. You will never ask me anything more than the two words? "

"Never! Never! "

"You will never put them to a bad use, if I say them? "

"Never! Never! "

"Walter Wilding. "

The lady lays her face upon the nurse's breast, draws her close in her embrace with both arms, murmurs a blessing and the words, "Kiss him for me! " and is gone.

* * * * *

Day of the month and year, the first Sunday in October, one thousand eight hundred and forty-seven. London Time by the great clock of Saint Paul's, half-past one in the afternoon. The clock of the Hospital for Foundling Children is well up with the Cathedral to-day. Service in the chapel is over, and the Foundling children are at dinner.

There are numerous lookers-on at the dinner, as the custom is. There are two or three governors, whole families from the congregation, smaller groups of both sexes, individual stragglers of various degrees. The bright autumnal sun strikes freshly into the wards; and the heavy-framed windows through which it shines, and the panelled walls on which it strikes, are such windows and such walls as pervade Hogarth's pictures. The girls' refectory (including that of the younger children) is the principal attraction. Neat attendants silently glide about the orderly and silent tables; the lookers-on move or stop as the fancy takes them; comments in whispers on face such a number from such a window are not unfrequent; many of the faces are of a character to fix attention. Some of the visitors from the outside public are accustomed visitors. They have established a speaking acquaintance with the occupants of particular seats at the tables, and halt at those points to bend down and say a word or two. It is no disparagement to their kindness that those points are generally points where personal attractions are. The monotony of the long spacious rooms and the double lines of faces is agreeably relieved by these incidents, although so slight.

A veiled lady, who has no companion, goes among the company. It would seem that curiosity and opportunity have never brought her there before. She has the air of being a little troubled by the sight, and, as she goes the length of the tables, it is with a hesitating step and an uneasy manner. At length she comes to the refectory of the boys. They are so much less popular than the girls that it is bare of visitors when she looks in at the doorway.

But just within the doorway, chances to stand, inspecting, an elderly female attendant: some order of matron or housekeeper. To whom the lady addresses natural questions: As, how many boys? At what age are they usually put out in life? Do they often take a fancy to the sea? So, lower and lower in tone until the lady puts the question: "Which is Walter Wilding? "

Attendant's head shaken. Against the rules.

"You know which is Walter Wilding? "

So keenly does the attendant feel the closeness with which the lady's eyes examine her face, that she keeps her own eyes fast upon the floor, lest by wandering in the right direction they should betray her.

"I know which is Walter Wilding, but it is not my place, ma'am, to tell names to visitors. "

"But you can show me without telling me. "

The lady's hand moves quietly to the attendant's hand. Pause and silence.

"I am going to pass round the tables, " says the lady's interlocutor, without seeming to address her. "Follow me with your eyes. The boy that I stop at and speak to, will not matter to you. But the boy that I touch, will be Walter Wilding. Say nothing more to me, and move a little away. "

Quickly acting on the hint, the lady passes on into the room, and looks about her. After a few moments, the attendant, in a staid official way, walks down outside the line of tables commencing on her left hand. She goes the whole length of the line, turns, and comes back on the inside. Very slightly glancing in the lady's direction, she stops, bends forward, and speaks. The boy whom she addresses, lifts his head and replies. Good humouredly and easily, as she listens to what he says, she lays her hand upon the shoulder of the next boy on his right. That the action may be well noted, she keeps her hand on the shoulder while speaking in return, and pats it twice or thrice before moving away. She completes her tour of the tables, touching no one else, and passes out by a door at the opposite end of the long room.

Dinner is done, and the lady, too, walks down outside the line of tables commencing on her left hand, goes the whole length of the line, turns, and comes back on the inside. Other people have strolled in, fortunately for her, and stand sprinkled about. She lifts her veil, and, stopping at the touched boy, asks how old he is?

"I am twelve, ma'am, " he answers, with his bright eyes fixed on hers.

"Are you well and happy? "

"Yes, ma'am. "

"May you take these sweetmeats from my hand? "

"If you please to give them to me. "

In stooping low for the purpose, the lady touches the boy's face with her forehead and with her hair. Then, lowering her veil again, she passes on, and passes out without looking back.

## ACT I.

## THE CURTAIN RISES

In a court-yard in the City of London, which was No Thoroughfare either for vehicles or foot-passengers; a court-yard diverging from a steep, a slippery, and a winding street connecting Tower Street with the Middlesex shore of the Thames; stood the place of business of Wilding & Co., Wine Merchants. Probably as a jocose acknowledgment of the obstructive character of this main approach, the point nearest to its base at which one could take the river (if so inodorously minded) bore the appellation Break-Neck-Stairs. The court-yard itself had likewise been descriptively entitled in old time, Cripple Corner.

Years before the year one thousand eight hundred and sixty-one, people had left off taking boat at Break-Neck-Stairs, and watermen had ceased to ply there. The slimy little causeway had dropped into the river by a slow process of suicide, and two or three stumps of piles and a rusty iron mooring-ring were all that remained of the departed Break-Neck glories. Sometimes, indeed, a laden coal barge would bump itself into the place, and certain laborious heavers, seemingly mud-engendered, would arise, deliver the cargo in the neighbourhood, shove off, and vanish; but at most times the only commerce of Break-Neck-Stairs arose out of the conveyance of casks and bottles, both full and empty, both to and from the cellars of Wilding & Co., Wine Merchants. Even that commerce was but occasional, and through three-fourths of its rising tides the dirty indecorous drab of a river would come solitarily oozing and lapping at the rusty ring, as if it had heard of the Doge and the Adriatic, and wanted to be married to the great conserver of its filthiness, the Right Honourable the Lord Mayor.

Some two hundred and fifty yards on the right, up the opposite hill (approaching it from the low ground of Break-Neck-Stairs) was Cripple Corner. There was a pump in Cripple Corner, there was a tree in Cripple Corner. All Cripple Corner belonged to Wilding and Co., Wine Merchants. Their cellars burrowed under it, their mansion towered over it. It really had been a mansion in the days when merchants inhabited the City, and had a ceremonious shelter to the doorway without visible support, like the sounding-board over an old pulpit. It had also a number of long narrow strips of window, so disposed in its grave brick front as to render it symmetrically ugly. It had also, on its roof, a cupola with a bell in it.

"When a man at five-and-twenty can put his hat on, and can say 'this hat covers the owner of this property and of the business which is transacted on this property, ' I consider, Mr. Bintrey, that, without being boastful, he may be allowed to be deeply thankful. I don't know how it may appear to you, but so it appears to me. "

Thus Mr. Walter Wilding to his man of law, in his own counting-house; taking his hat down from its peg to suit the action to the word, and hanging it up again when he had done so, not to overstep the modesty of nature.

An innocent, open-speaking, unused-looking man, Mr. Walter Wilding, with a remarkably pink and white complexion, and a figure much too bulky for so young a man, though of a good stature. With crispy curling brown hair, and amiable bright blue eyes. An extremely communicative man: a man with whom loquacity was the irrestrainable outpouring of contentment and gratitude. Mr. Bintrey, on the other hand, a cautious man, with twinkling beads of eyes in a large overhanging bald head, who inwardly but intensely enjoyed the comicality of openness of speech, or hand, or heart.

"Yes, " said Mr. Bintrey. "Yes. Ha, ha! "

A decanter, two wine-glasses, and a plate of biscuits, stood on the desk.

"You like this forty-five year old port-wine? " said Mr. Wilding.

"Like it? " repeated Mr. Bintrey. "Rather, sir! "

"It's from the best corner of our best forty-five year old bin, " said Mr. Wilding.

"Thank you, sir, " said Mr. Bintrey. "It's most excellent. "

He laughed again, as he held up his glass and ogled it, at the highly ludicrous idea of giving away such wine.

"And now, " said Wilding, with a childish enjoyment in the discussion of affairs, "I think we have got everything straight, Mr. Bintrey. "

"Everything straight, " said Bintrey.

"A partner secured —"

"Partner secured, " said Bintrey.

"A housekeeper advertised for —"

"Housekeeper advertised for, " said Bintrey, "'apply personally at Cripple Corner, Great Tower Street, from ten to twelve' — to-morrow, by the bye. "

"My late dear mother's affairs wound up —"

"Wound up, " said Bintrey.

"And all charges paid. "

"And all charges paid, " said Bintrey, with a chuckle: probably occasioned by the droll circumstance that they had been paid without a haggle.

"The mention of my late dear mother, " Mr. Wilding continued, his eyes filling with tears and his pocket-handkerchief drying them, "unmans me still, Mr. Bintrey. You know how I loved her; you (her lawyer) know how she loved me. The utmost love of mother and child was cherished between us, and we never experienced one moment's division or unhappiness from the time when she took me under her care. Thirteen years in all! Thirteen years under my late dear mother's care, Mr. Bintrey, and eight of them her confidentially acknowledged son! You know the story, Mr. Bintrey, who but you, sir! " Mr. Wilding sobbed and dried his eyes, without attempt at concealment, during these remarks.

Mr. Bintrey enjoyed his comical port, and said, after rolling it in his mouth: "I know the story. "

"My late dear mother, Mr. Bintrey, " pursued the wine-merchant, "had been deeply deceived, and had cruelly suffered. But on that subject my late dear mother's lips were for ever sealed. By whom deceived, or under what circumstances, Heaven only knows. My late dear mother never betrayed her betrayer. "

"She had made up her mind, " said Mr. Bintrey, again turning his wine on his palate, "and she could hold her peace. " An amused twinkle in his eyes pretty plainly added—"A devilish deal better than *you* ever will! "

"'Honour, '" said Mr. Wilding, sobbing as he quoted from the Commandments, "'thy father and thy mother, that thy days may be long in the land. ' When I was in the Foundling, Mr. Bintrey, I was at such a loss how to do it, that I apprehended my days would be short in the land. But I afterwards came to honour my mother deeply, profoundly. And I honour and revere her memory. For seven happy years, Mr. Bintrey, " pursued Wilding, still with the same innocent catching in his breath, and the same unabashed tears, "did my excellent mother article me to my predecessors in this business, Pebbleson Nephew. Her affectionate forethought likewise apprenticed me to the Vintners' Company, and made me in time a free Vintner, and—and—everything else that the best of mothers could desire. When I came of age, she bestowed her inherited share in this business upon me; it was her money that afterwards bought out Pebbleson Nephew, and painted in Wilding and Co. ; it was she who left me everything she possessed, but the mourning ring you wear. And yet, Mr. Bintrey, " with a fresh burst of honest affection, "she is no more. It is little over half a year since she came into the Corner to read on that door-post with her own eyes, WILDING AND CO., WINE MERCHANTS. And yet she is no more! "

"Sad. But the common lot, Mr. Wilding, " observed Bintrey. "At some time or other we must all be no more. " He placed the forty-five year old port- wine in the universal condition, with a relishing sigh.

"So now, Mr. Bintrey, " pursued Wilding, putting away his pocket-handkerchief, and smoothing his eyelids with his fingers, "now that I can no longer show my love and honour for the dear parent to whom my heart was mysteriously turned by Nature when she first spoke to me, a strange lady, I sitting at our Sunday dinner-table in the Foundling, I can at least show that I am not ashamed of having been a Foundling, and that I, who never knew a father of my own, wish to be a father to all in my employment. Therefore, " continued

Wilding, becoming enthusiastic in his loquacity, "therefore, I want a thoroughly good housekeeper to undertake this dwelling-house of Wilding and Co., Wine Merchants, Cripple Corner, so that I may restore in it some of the old relations betwixt employer and employed! So that I may live in it on the spot where my money is made! So that I may daily sit at the head of the table at which the people in my employment eat together, and may eat of the same roast and boiled, and drink of the same beer! So that the people in my employment may lodge under the same roof with me! So that we may one and all—I beg your pardon, Mr. Bintrey, but that old singing in my head has suddenly come on, and I shall feel obliged if you will lead me to the pump. "

Alarmed by the excessive pinkness of his client, Mr. Bintrey lost not a moment in leading him forth into the court-yard. It was easily done; for the counting-house in which they talked together opened on to it, at one side of the dwelling-house. There the attorney pumped with a will, obedient to a sign from the client, and the client laved his head and face with both hands, and took a hearty drink. After these remedies, he declared himself much better.

"Don't let your good feelings excite you, " said Bintrey, as they returned to the counting-house, and Mr. Wilding dried himself on a jack-towel behind an inner door.

"No, no. I won't, " he returned, looking out of the towel. "I won't. I have not been confused, have I? "

"Not at all. Perfectly clear. "

"Where did I leave off, Mr. Bintrey? "

"Well, you left off—but I wouldn't excite myself, if I was you, by taking it up again just yet. "

"I'll take care. I'll take care. The singing in my head came on at where, Mr. Bintrey? "

"At roast, and boiled, and beer, " answered the lawyer, — "prompting lodging under the same roof—and one and all—"

"Ah! And one and all singing in the head together—"

"Do you know, I really *would not* let my good feelings excite me, if I was you, " hinted the lawyer again, anxiously. "Try some more pump. "

"No occasion, no occasion. All right, Mr. Bintrey. And one and all forming a kind of family! You see, Mr. Bintrey, I was not used in my childhood to that sort of individual existence which most individuals have led, more or less, in their childhood. After that time I became absorbed in my late dear mother. Having lost her, I find that I am more fit for being one of a body than one by myself one. To be that, and at the same time to do my duty to those dependent on me, and attach them to me, has a patriarchal and pleasant air about it. I don't know how it may appear to you, Mr Bintrey, but so it appears to me. "

"It is not I who am all-important in the case, but you, " returned Bintrey. "Consequently, how it may appear to me is of very small importance. "

"It appears to me, " said Mr. Wilding, in a glow, "hopeful, useful, delightful! "

"Do you know, " hinted the lawyer again, "I really would not ex —"

"I am not going to. Then there's Handel. "

"There's who? " asked Bintrey.

"Handel, Mozart, Haydn, Kent, Purcell, Doctor Arne, Greene, Mendelssohn. I know the choruses to those anthems by heart. Foundling Chapel Collection. Why shouldn't we learn them together? "

"Who learn them together? " asked the lawyer, rather shortly.

"Employer and employed. "

"Ay, ay, " returned Bintrey, mollified; as if he had half expected the answer to be, Lawyer and client. "That's another thing. "

"Not another thing, Mr. Bintrey! The same thing. A part of the bond among us. We will form a Choir in some quiet church near the Corner here, and, having sung together of a Sunday with a relish, we will come home and take an early dinner together with a relish. The object that I have at heart now is, to get this system well in action without delay, so that my new partner may find it founded when he enters on his partnership. "

"All good be with it! " exclaimed Bintrey, rising. "May it prosper! Is Joey Ladle to take a share in Handel, Mozart, Haydn, Kent, Purcell, Doctor Arne, Greene, and Mendelssohn?

"I hope so. "

"I wish them all well out of it, " returned Bintrey, with much heartiness. "Good-bye, sir. "

They shook hands and parted. Then (first knocking with his knuckles for leave) entered to Mr. Wilding from a door of communication between his private counting-house and that in which his clerks sat, the Head Cellarman of the cellars of Wilding and Co., Wine Merchants, and erst Head Cellarman of the cellars of Pebbleson Nephew. The Joey Ladle in question. A slow and ponderous man, of the drayman order of human architecture, dressed in a corrugated suit and bibbed apron, apparently a composite of door-mat and rhinoceros-hide.

"Respecting this same boarding and lodging, Young Master Wilding, " said he.

"Yes, Joey? "

"Speaking for myself, Young Master Wilding—and I never did speak and I never do speak for no one else—I don't want no boarding nor yet no lodging. But if you wish to board me and to lodge me, take me. I can peck as well as most men. Where I peck ain't so high a object with me as What I peck. Nor even so high a object with me as How Much I peck. Is all to live in the house, Young Master Wilding? The two other cellarmen, the three porters, the two 'prentices, and the odd men? "

"Yes. I hope we shall all be an united family, Joey. "

"Ah! " said Joey. "I hope they may be. "

"They? Rather say we, Joey. "

Joey Ladle shook his held. "Don't look to me to make we on it, Young Master Wilding, not at my time of life and under the circumstances which has formed my disposition. I have said to Pebbleson Nephew many a time, when they have said to me, 'Put a livelier face upon it, Joey'—I have said to them, 'Gentlemen, it is all wery well for you that has been accustomed to take your wine into your systems by the conwivial channel of your throttles, to put a lively face upon it; but, ' I says, 'I have been accustomed to take *my* wine in at the pores of the skin, and, took that way, it acts different. It acts depressing. It's one thing, gentlemen, ' I says to Pebbleson Nephew, 'to charge your glasses in a dining-room with a Hip Hurrah and a Jolly Companions Every One, and it's another thing to be charged yourself, through the pores, in a low dark cellar and a mouldy atmosphere. It makes all the difference betwixt bubbles and wapours, ' I tells Pebbleson Nephew. And so it do. I've been a cellarman my life through, with my mind fully given to the business. What's the consequence? I'm as muddled a man as lives—you won't find a muddleder man than me—nor yet you won't find my equal in molloncolly. Sing of Filling the bumper fair, Every drop you sprinkle, O'er the brow of care, Smooths away a wrinkle? Yes. P'raps so. But try filling yourself through the pores, underground, when you don't want to it! "

"I am sorry to hear this, Joey. I had even thought that you might join a singing-class in the house. "

"Me, sir? No, no, Young Master Wilding, you won't catch Joey Ladle muddling the Armony. A pecking-machine, sir, is all that I am capable of proving myself, out of my cellars; but that you're welcome to, if you think it is worth your while to keep such a thing on your premises. "

"I do, Joey. "

"Say no more, sir. The Business's word is my law. And you're a going to take Young Master George Vendale partner into the old Business? "

"I am, Joey. "

"More changes, you see! But don't change the name of the Firm again. Don't do it, Young Master Wilding. It was bad luck enough to make it Yourself and Co. Better by far have left it Pebbleson Nephew that good luck always stuck to. You should never change luck when it's good, sir. "

"At all events, I have no intention of changing the name of the House again, Joey. "

"Glad to hear it, and wish you good-day, Young Master Wilding. But you had better by half, " muttered Joey Ladle inaudibly, as he closed the door and shook his head, "have let the name alone from the first. You had better by half have followed the luck instead of crossing it. "

## ENTER THE HOUSEKEEPER

The wine merchant sat in his dining-room next morning, to receive the personal applicants for the vacant post in his establishment. It was an old-fashioned wainscoted room; the panels ornamented with festoons of flowers carved in wood; with an oaken floor, a well-worn Turkey carpet, and dark mahogany furniture, all of which had seen service and polish under Pebbleson Nephew. The great sideboard had assisted at many business-dinners given by Pebbleson Nephew to their connection, on the principle of throwing sprats overboard to catch whales; and Pebbleson Nephew's comprehensive three-sided plate-warmer, made to fit the whole front of the large fireplace, kept watch beneath it over a sarcophagus- shaped cellaret that had in its time held many a dozen of Pebbleson Nephew's wine. But the little rubicund old bachelor with a pigtail, whose portrait was over the sideboard (and who could easily be identified as decidedly Pebbleson and decidedly not Nephew), had retired into another sarcophagus, and the plate-warmer had grown as cold as he. So, the golden and black griffins that supported the candelabra, with black balls in their mouths at the end of gilded chains, looked as if in their old age they had lost all heart for playing at ball, and were dolefully exhibiting their chains in the Missionary line of inquiry, whether they had not earned emancipation by this time, and were not griffins and brothers.

Such a Columbus of a morning was the summer morning, that it discovered Cripple Corner. The light and warmth pierced in at the open windows, and irradiated the picture of a lady hanging over the chimney-piece, the only other decoration of the walls.

"My mother at five-and-twenty, " said Mr. Wilding to himself, as his eyes enthusiastically followed the light to the portrait's face, "I hang up here, in order that visitors may admire my mother in the bloom of her youth and beauty. My mother at fifty I hang in the seclusion of my own chamber, as a remembrance sacred to me. O! It's you, Jarvis! "

These latter words he addressed to a clerk who had tapped at the door, and now looked in.

"Yes, sir. I merely wished to mention that it's gone ten, sir, and that there are several females in the Counting-house. "

"Dear me! " said the wine-merchant, deepening in the pink of his complexion and whitening in the white, "are there several? So many as several? I had better begin before there are more. I'll see them one by one, Jarvis, in the order of their arrival. "

Hastily entrenching himself in his easy-chair at the table behind a great inkstand, having first placed a chair on the other side of the table opposite his own seat, Mr. Wilding entered on his task with considerable trepidation.

He ran the gauntlet that must be run on any such occasion. There were the usual species of profoundly unsympathetic women, and the usual species of much too sympathetic women. There were buccaneering widows who came to seize him, and who griped umbrellas under their arms, as if each umbrella were he, and each griper had got him. There were towering maiden ladies who had seen better days, and who came armed with clerical testimonials to their theology, as if he were Saint Peter with his keys. There were gentle maiden ladies who came to marry him. There were professional housekeepers, like non-commissioned officers, who put him through his domestic exercise, instead of submitting themselves to catechism. There were languid invalids, to whom salary was not so much an object as the comforts of a private hospital. There were sensitive creatures who burst into tears on being addressed, and had to be restored with glasses of cold water. There were some respondents who came two together, a highly promising one and a wholly unpromising one: of whom the promising one answered all questions charmingly, until it would at last appear that she was not a candidate at all, but only the friend of the unpromising one, who had glowered in absolute silence and apparent injury.

At last, when the good wine-merchant's simple heart was failing him, there entered an applicant quite different from all the rest. A woman, perhaps fifty, but looking younger, with a face remarkable for placid cheerfulness, and a manner no less remarkable for its quiet expression of equability of temper. Nothing in her dress could have been changed to her advantage. Nothing in the noiseless self-possession of her manner could have been changed to her advantage. Nothing could have been in better unison with both, than her voice when she answered the question: "What name shall I have the pleasure of noting down? " with the words, "My name is Sarah Goldstraw. Mrs. Goldstraw. My husband has been dead many years, and we had no family. "

Half-a-dozen questions had scarcely extracted as much to the purpose from any one else. The voice dwelt so agreeably on Mr. Wilding's ear as he made his note, that he was rather long about it. When he looked up again, Mrs. Goldstraw's glance had naturally gone round the room, and now returned to him from the chimney-piece. Its expression was one of frank readiness to be questioned, and to answer straight.

"You will excuse my asking you a few questions? " said the modest wine- merchant.

"O, surely, sir. Or I should have no business here. "

"Have you filled the station of housekeeper before? "

"Only once. I have lived with the same widow lady for twelve years. Ever since I lost my husband. She was an invalid, and is lately dead: which is the occasion of my now wearing black. "

"I do not doubt that she has left you the best credentials? " said Mr. Wilding.

"I hope I may say, the very best. I thought it would save trouble, sir, if I wrote down the name and address of her representatives, and brought it with me. " Laying a card on the table.

"You singularly remind me, Mrs. Goldstraw, " said Wilding, taking the card beside him, "of a manner and tone of voice that I was once acquainted with. Not of an individual—I feel sure of that, though I cannot recall what it is I have in my mind—but of a general bearing. I ought to add, it was a kind and pleasant one. "

She smiled, as she rejoined: "At least, I am very glad of that, sir. "

"Yes, " said the wine-merchant, thoughtfully repeating his last phrase, with a momentary glance at his future housekeeper, "it was a kind and pleasant one. But that is the most I can make of it. Memory is sometimes like a half-forgotten dream. I don't know how it may appear to you, Mrs. Goldstraw, but so it appears to me. "

Probably it appeared to Mrs. Goldstraw in a similar light, for she quietly assented to the proposition. Mr. Wilding then offered to put himself at once in communication with the gentlemen named upon the card: a firm of proctors in Doctors' Commons. To this, Mrs. Goldstraw thankfully assented. Doctors' Commons not being far off, Mr. Wilding suggested the feasibility of Mrs. Goldstraw's looking in again, say in three hours' time. Mrs. Goldstraw readily undertook to do so. In fine, the result of Mr. Wilding's inquiries being eminently satisfactory, Mrs. Goldstraw was that afternoon engaged (on her own perfectly fair terms) to come to-morrow and set up her rest as housekeeper in Cripple Corner.

## THE HOUSEKEEPER SPEAKS

On the next day Mrs. Goldstraw arrived, to enter on her domestic duties.

Having settled herself in her own room, without troubling the servants, and without wasting time, the new housekeeper announced herself as waiting to be favoured with any instructions which her master might wish to give her. The wine-merchant received Mrs. Goldstraw in the dining- room, in which he had seen her on the previous day; and, the usual preliminary civilities having passed on either side, the two sat down to take counsel together on the affairs of the house.

"About the meals, sir? " said Mrs. Goldstraw. "Have I a large, or a small, number to provide for? "

"If I can carry out a certain old-fashioned plan of mine, " replied Mr. Wilding, "you will have a large number to provide for. I am a lonely single man, Mrs. Goldstraw; and I hope to live with all the persons in my employment as if they were members of my family. Until that time comes, you will only have me, and the new partner whom I expect immediately, to provide for. What my partner's habits may be, I cannot yet say. But I may describe myself as a man of regular hours, with an invariable appetite that you may depend upon to an ounce. "

"About breakfast, sir? " asked Mrs. Goldstraw. "Is there anything particular—? "

She hesitated, and left the sentence unfinished. Her eyes turned slowly away from her master, and looked towards the chimney-piece. If she had been a less excellent and experienced housekeeper, Mr. Wilding might have fancied that her attention was beginning to wander at the very outset of the interview.

"Eight o'clock is my breakfast-hour, " he resumed. "It is one of my virtues to be never tired of broiled bacon, and it is one of my vices to be habitually suspicious of the freshness of eggs. " Mrs. Goldstraw looked back at him, still a little divided between her master's chimney- piece and her master. "I take tea, " Mr. Wilding went on; "and I am perhaps rather nervous and fidgety about drinking it, within a certain time after it is made. If my tea stands too long —"

He hesitated, on his side, and left the sentence unfinished. If he had not been engaged in discussing a subject of such paramount interest to himself as his breakfast, Mrs. Goldstraw might have fancied that his attention was beginning to wander at the very outset of the interview.

"If your tea stands too long, sir—? " said the housekeeper, politely taking up her master's lost thread.

"If my tea stands too long, " repeated the wine-merchant mechanically, his mind getting farther and farther away from his breakfast, and his eyes fixing themselves more and more inquiringly on his housekeeper's face. "If my tea—Dear, dear me, Mrs. Goldstraw! what *is* the manner and tone of voice that you remind me of? It strikes me even more strongly to-day, than it did when I saw you yesterday. What can it be? "

"What can it be? " repeated Mrs. Goldstraw.

She said the words, evidently thinking while she spoke them of something else. The wine-merchant, still looking at her inquiringly, observed that her eyes wandered towards the chimney-piece once more. They fixed on the portrait of his mother, which hung there, and looked at it with that slight contraction of the brow which accompanies a scarcely conscious effort of memory. Mr. Wilding remarked.

"My late dear mother, when she was five-and-twenty. "

Mrs. Goldstraw thanked him with a movement of the head for being at the pains to explain the picture, and said, with a cleared brow, that it was the portrait of a very beautiful lady.

Mr. Wilding, falling back into his former perplexity, tried once more to recover that lost recollection, associated so closely, and yet so undiscoverably, with his new housekeeper's voice and manner.

"Excuse my asking you a question which has nothing to do with me or my breakfast, " he said. "May I inquire if you have ever occupied any other situation than the situation of housekeeper? "

"O yes, sir. I began life as one of the nurses at the Foundling. "

"Why, that's it! " cried the wine-merchant, pushing back his chair. "By heaven! Their manner is the manner you remind me of! "

In an astonished look at him, Mrs. Goldstraw changed colour, checked herself, turned her eyes upon the ground, and sat still and silent.

"What is the matter? " asked Mr. Wilding.

"Do I understand that you were in the Foundling, sir? "

"Certainly. I am not ashamed to own it. "

"Under the name you now bear? "

"Under the name of Walter Wilding. "

"And the lady—? " Mrs. Goldstraw stopped short with a look at the portrait which was now unmistakably a look of alarm.

"You mean my mother, " interrupted Mr. Wilding.

"Your—mother, " repeated the housekeeper, a little constrainedly, "removed you from the Foundling? At what age, sir? "

"At between eleven and twelve years old. It's quite a romantic adventure, Mrs. Goldstraw. "

He told the story of the lady having spoken to him, while he sat at dinner with the other boys in the Foundling, and of all that had followed in his innocently communicative way. "My poor mother could never have discovered me, " he added, "if she had not met with one of the matrons who pitied her. The matron consented to touch the boy whose name was 'Walter Wilding' as she went round the dinner-tables—and so my mother discovered me again, after having parted from me as an infant at the Foundling doors. "

At those words Mrs. Goldstraw's hand, resting on the table, dropped helplessly into her lap. She sat, looking at her new master, with a face that had turned deadly pale, and with eyes that expressed an unutterable dismay.

"What does this mean? " asked the wine-merchant. "Stop! " he cried. "Is there something else in the past time which I ought to associate with you? I remember my mother telling me of another person at the Foundling, to whose kindness she owed a debt of gratitude. When she first parted with me, as an infant, one of the nurses informed her of the name that had been given to me in the institution. You were that nurse? "

"God forgive me, sir—I was that nurse! "

"God forgive you? "

"We had better get back, sir (if I may make so bold as to say so), to my duties in the house, " said Mrs. Goldstraw. "Your breakfast-hour is eight. Do you lunch, or dine, in the middle of the day? "

The excessive pinkness which Mr. Bintrey had noticed in his client's face began to appear there once more. Mr. Wilding put his hand to his head, and mastered some momentary confusion in that quarter, before he spoke again.

"Mrs. Goldstraw, " he said, "you are concealing something from me! "

The housekeeper obstinately repeated, "Please to favour me, sir, by saying whether you lunch, or dine, in the middle of the day? "

"I don't know what I do in the middle of the day. I can't enter into my household affairs, Mrs. Goldstraw, till I know why you regret an act of kindness to my mother, which she always spoke of gratefully to the end of her life. You are not doing me a service by your silence. You are agitating me, you are alarming me, you are bringing on the singing in my head. "

His hand went up to his head again, and the pink in his face deepened by a shade or two.

"It's hard, sir, on just entering your service, " said the housekeeper, "to say what may cost me the loss of your good will. Please to remember, end how it may, that I only speak because you have insisted on my speaking, and because I see that I am alarming you by my silence. When I told the poor lady, whose portrait you have got there, the name by which her infant was christened in the Foundling, I allowed myself to forget my duty, and dreadful consequences, I am afraid, have followed from it. I'll tell you the truth, as plainly as I can. A few months from the time when I had informed the lady of her baby's name, there came to our institution in the country another lady (a stranger), whose object was to adopt one of our children. She brought the needful permission with her, and after looking at a great many of the children, without being able to make up her mind, she took a sudden fancy to one of the babies — a boy—under my care. Try, pray try, to compose yourself, sir! It's no use disguising it any longer. The child the stranger took away was the child of that lady whose portrait hangs there! "

Mr. Wilding started to his feet. "Impossible! " he cried out, vehemently. "What are you talking about? What absurd story are you telling me now? There's her portrait! Haven't I told you so already? The portrait of my mother! "

"When that unhappy lady removed you from the Foundling, in after years, " said Mrs. Goldstraw, gently, "she was the victim, and you were the victim, sir, of a dreadful mistake. "

He dropped back into his chair. "The room goes round with me, " he said. "My head! my head! " The housekeeper rose in alarm, and opened the windows. Before she could get to the door to call for help, a sudden burst of tears relieved the oppression which had at first almost appeared to threaten his life. He signed entreatingly to Mrs. Goldstraw not to leave him. She waited until the paroxysm of weeping had worn itself out. He raised his head as he recovered himself, and looked at her with the angry unreasoning suspicion of a weak man.

"Mistake? " he said, wildly repeating her last word. "How do I know you are not mistaken yourself? "

"There is no hope that I am mistaken, sir. I will tell you why, when you are better fit to hear it. "

"Now! now! "

The tone in which he spoke warned Mrs. Goldstraw that it would be cruel kindness to let him comfort himself a moment longer with the vain hope that she might be wrong. A few words more would end it, and those few words she determined to speak.

"I have told you, " she said, "that the child of the lady whose portrait hangs there, was adopted in its infancy, and taken away by a stranger. I am as certain of what I say as that I am now sitting here, obliged to distress you, sir, sorely against my will. Please to carry your mind on, now, to about three months after that time. I was then at the Foundling, in London, waiting to take some children to our institution in the country. There was a question that day about naming an infant—a boy—who had just been received. We generally named them out of the Directory. On this occasion, one of the gentlemen who managed the Hospital happened to be looking over the Register. He noticed that the name of the baby who had been adopted ('Walter Wilding') was scratched out—for the reason, of course, that the child had been removed for good from our care. 'Here's a name to let, ' he said. 'Give it to the new foundling who has been received to-day. ' The name was given, and the child was christened. You, sir, were that child. "

The wine-merchant's head dropped on his breast. "I was that child! " he said to himself, trying helplessly to fix the idea in his mind. "I was that child! "

"Not very long after you had been received into the Institution, sir, " pursued Mrs. Goldstraw, "I left my situation there, to be married. If you will remember that, and if you can give your mind to it, you will see for yourself how the mistake happened. Between eleven and twelve years passed before the lady, whom you have believed to be your mother, returned to the Foundling, to find her son, and to remove him to her own home. The lady only knew that her infant had been called 'Walter Wilding. ' The matron who took pity on her, could but point out the only 'Walter Wilding' known in the Institution. I, who might have set the matter right, was far away from the Foundling and all that belonged to it. There was nothing — there was really nothing that could prevent this terrible mistake from taking place. I feel for you — I do indeed, sir! You must think — and with reason — that it was in an evil hour that I came here (innocently enough, I'm sure), to apply for your housekeeper's place. I feel as if I was to blame — I feel as if I ought to have had more self-command. If I had only been able to keep my face from showing you what that portrait and what your own words put into my mind, you need never, to your dying day, have known what you know now. "

Mr. Wilding looked up suddenly. The inbred honesty of the man rose in protest against the housekeeper's last words. His mind seemed to steady itself, for the moment, under the shock that had fallen on it.

"Do you mean to say that you would have concealed this from me if you could? " he exclaimed.

"I hope I should always tell the truth, sir, if I was asked, " said Mrs. Goldstraw. "And I know it is better for *me* that I should not have a secret of this sort weighing on my mind. But is it better for *you*? What use can it serve now — ? "

"What use? Why, good Lord! if your story is true — "

"Should I have told it, sir, as I am now situated, if it had not been true? "

"I beg your pardon, " said the wine-merchant. "You must make allowance for me. This dreadful discovery is something I can't realise even yet. We loved each other so dearly — I felt so fondly that I was her son. She died, Mrs. Goldstraw, in my arms — she died blessing me as only a mother *could* have blessed me. And now, after all these years, to be told she was *not* my mother! O me, O me! I don't know what I am saying! " he cried, as the impulse of self-control under which he had spoken a moment since, flickered, and died out. "It was not this dreadful grief—it was something else that I had it in my mind to speak of. Yes, yes. You surprised me—you wounded me just now. You talked as if you would have hidden this from me, if you could. Don't talk in that way again. It would have been a crime to have hidden it. You mean well, I know. I don't want to distress you—you are a kind-hearted woman. But you don't remember what my position is. She left me all that I possess, in the firm persuasion that I was her son. I am not her son. I have taken the place, I have innocently got the inheritance of another man. He must be found! How do I know he is not at this moment in misery, without bread to eat? He must be found! My only hope of bearing up against the shock that has fallen on me, is the hope of doing something which *she* would have approved. You must know more, Mrs. Goldstraw, than you have told me yet. Who was the stranger who adopted the child? You must have heard the lady's name? "

"I never heard it, sir. I have never seen her, or heard of her, since. "

"Did she say nothing when she took the child away? Search your memory. She must have said something. "

"Only one thing, sir, that I can remember. It was a miserably bad season, that year; and many of the children were suffering from it. When she took the baby away, the lady said to me, laughing, 'Don't be alarmed about his health. He will be brought up in a better climate than this—I am going to take him to Switzerland. '"

"To Switzerland? What part of Switzerland? "

"She didn't say, sir. "

"Only that faint clue! " said Mr. Wilding. "And a quarter of a century has passed since the child was taken away! What am I to do? "

"I hope you won't take offence at my freedom, sir, " said Mrs. Goldstraw; "but why should you distress yourself about what is to be done? He may not be alive now, for anything you know. And, if he is alive, it's not likely he can be in any distress. The, lady who adopted him was a bred and born lady—it was easy to see that. And she must have satisfied them at the Foundling that she could provide for the child, or they would never have let her take him away. If I was in your place, sir—please to excuse my saying so—I should

25

comfort myself with remembering that I had loved that poor lady whose portrait you have got there—truly loved her as my mother, and that she had truly loved me as her son. All she gave to you, she gave for the sake of that love. It never altered while she lived; and it won't alter, I'm sure, as long as *you* live. How can you have a better right, sir, to keep what you have got than that? "

Mr. Wilding's immovable honesty saw the fallacy in his housekeeper's point of view at a glance.

"You don't understand me, " he said. "It's *because* I loved her that I feel it a duty—a sacred duty—to do justice to her son. If he is a living man, I must find him: for my own sake, as well as for his. I shall break down under this dreadful trial, unless I employ myself—actively, instantly employ myself—in doing what my conscience tells me ought to be done. I must speak to my lawyer; I must set my lawyer at work before I sleep to-night. " He approached a tube in the wall of the room, and called down through it to the office below. "Leave me for a little, Mrs. Goldstraw, " he resumed; "I shall be more composed, I shall be better able to speak to you later in the day. We shall get on well—I hope we shall get on well together—in spite of what has happened. It isn't your fault; I know it isn't your fault. There! there! shake hands; and—and do the best you can in the house—I can't talk about it now. "

The door opened as Mrs. Goldstraw advanced towards it; and Mr. Jarvis appeared.

"Send for Mr. Bintrey, " said the wine-merchant. "Say I want to see him directly. "

The clerk unconsciously suspended the execution of the order, by announcing "Mr. Vendale, " and showing in the new partner in the firm of Wilding and Co.

"Pray excuse me for one moment, George Vendale, " said Wilding. "I have a word to say to Jarvis. Send for Mr. Bintrey, " he repeated—"send at once. "

Mr. Jarvis laid a letter on the table before he left the room.

"From our correspondents at Neuchatel, I think, sir. The letter has got the Swiss postmark. "

## NEW CHARACTERS ON THE SCENE

The words, "The Swiss Postmark, " following so soon upon the housekeeper's reference to Switzerland, wrought Mr. Wilding's agitation to such a remarkable height, that his new partner could not decently make a pretence of letting it pass unnoticed.

"Wilding, " he asked hurriedly, and yet stopping short and glancing around as if for some visible cause of his state of mind: "what is the matter? "

"My good George Vendale, " returned the wine-merchant, giving his hand with an appealing look, rather as if he wanted help to get over some obstacle, than as if he gave it in welcome or salutation: "my good George Vendale, so much is the matter, that I shall never be myself again. It is impossible that I can ever be myself again. For, in fact, I am not myself. "

The new partner, a brown-cheeked handsome fellow, of about his own age, with a quick determined eye and an impulsive manner, retorted with natural astonishment: "Not yourself? "

"Not what I supposed myself to be, " said Wilding.

"What, in the name of wonder, *did* you suppose yourself to be that you are not? " was the rejoinder, delivered with a cheerful frankness, inviting confidence from a more reticent man. "I may ask without impertinence, now that we are partners. "

"There again! " cried Wilding, leaning back in his chair, with a lost look at the other. "Partners! I had no right to come into this business. It was never meant for me. My mother never meant it should be mine. I mean, his mother meant it should be his—if I mean anything—or if I am anybody. "

"Come, come, " urged his partner, after a moment's pause, and taking possession of him with that calm confidence which inspires a strong nature when it honestly desires to aid a weak one. "Whatever has gone wrong, has gone wrong through no fault of yours, I am very sure. I was not in this counting-house with you, under the old *regime*, for three years, to doubt you, Wilding. We were not younger men than we are, together, for that. Let me begin our partnership by being a serviceable partner, and setting right whatever is wrong. Has that letter anything to do with it? "

"Hah! " said Wilding, with his hand to his temple. "There again! My head! I was forgetting the coincidence. The Swiss postmark. "

"At a second glance I see that the letter is unopened, so it is not very likely to have much to do with the matter, " said Vendale, with comforting composure. "Is it for you, or for us? "

"For us, " said Wilding.

"Suppose I open it and read it aloud, to get it out of our way? "

"Thank you, thank you. "

"The letter is only from our champagne-making friends, the house at Neuchatel. 'Dear Sir. We are in receipt of yours of the 28th ult., informing us that you have taken your Mr. Vendale into partnership, whereon we beg you to receive the assurance of our felicitations. Permit us to embrace the occasion of specially commanding to you M. Jules Obenreizer. ' Impossible! "

Wilding looked up in quick apprehension, and cried, "Eh? "

"Impossible sort of name, " returned his partner, slightly— "Obenreizer. '—Of specially commanding to you M. Jules Obenreizer, of Soho Square, London (north side), henceforth fully accredited as our agent, and who has already had the honour of making the acquaintance of your Mr. Vendale, in his (said M. Obenreizer's) native country, Switzerland. ' To be sure! pooh pooh, what have I been thinking of! I remember now; 'when  travelling with his niece. '"

"With his—? " Vendale had so slurred the last word, that Wilding had not heard it.

"When travelling with his Niece. Obenreizer's Niece, " said Vendale, in a somewhat superfluously lucid manner. "Niece of Obenreizer. (I met them in my first Swiss tour, travelled a little with them, and lost them for two years; met them again, my Swiss tour before last, and have lost them ever since. ) Obenreizer. Niece of Obenreizer. To be sure! Possible sort of name, after all! 'M. Obenreizer is in possession of our absolute confidence, and we do not doubt you will esteem his merits. ' Duly signed by the House, 'Defresnier et Cie. ' Very well. I undertake to see M. Obenreizer presently, and clear him out of the way. That clears the Swiss postmark out of the way. So now, my dear Wilding, tell me what I can clear out of *your* way, and I'll find a way to clear it. "

More than ready and grateful to be thus taken charge of, the honest wine- merchant wrung his partner's hand, and, beginning his tale by pathetically declaring himself an Impostor, told it.

"It was on this matter, no doubt, that you were sending for Bintrey when I came in? " said his partner, after reflecting.

"It was. "

"He has experience and a shrewd head; I shall be anxious to know his opinion. It is bold and hazardous in me to give you mine before I know his, but I am not good at holding back. Plainly, then, I do not see these circumstances as you see them. I do not see your position as you see it. As to your being an Impostor, my dear Wilding, that is simply absurd, because no man can be that without being a consenting party to an imposition. Clearly you never were so. As to your enrichment by the lady who believed you to be her son, and whom you were forced to believe, on her showing, to be your mother, consider whether that did not arise out of the personal relations between you. You gradually became much attached to her; she gradually became much attached to you. It was on you, personally you, as I see the case, that she conferred these worldly advantages; it was from her, personally her, that you took them. "

"She supposed me, " objected Wilding, shaking his head, "to have a natural claim upon her, which I had not. "

"I must admit that, " replied his partner, "to be true. But if she had made the discovery that you have made, six months before she died, do you think it would have cancelled the years you were together, and the tenderness that each of you had conceived for the other, each on increasing knowledge of the other? "

"What I think, " said Wilding, simply but stoutly holding to the bare fact, "can no more change the truth than it can bring down the sky.

The truth is that I stand possessed of what was meant for another man. "

"He may be dead, " said Vendale.

"He may be alive, " said Wilding. "And if he is alive, have I not—innocently, I grant you innocently—robbed him of enough? Have I not robbed him of all the happy time that I enjoyed in his stead? Have I not robbed him of the exquisite delight that filled my soul when that dear lady, " stretching his hand towards the picture, "told me she was my mother? Have I not robbed him of all the care she lavished on me? Have I not even robbed him of all the devotion and duty that I so proudly gave to her? Therefore it is that I ask myself, George Vendale, and I ask you, where is he? What has become of him? "

"Who can tell! "

"I must try to find out who can tell. I must institute inquiries. I must never desist from prosecuting inquiries. I will live upon the interest of my share—I ought to say his share—in this business, and will lay up the rest for him. When I find him, I may perhaps throw myself upon his generosity; but I will yield up all to him. I will, I swear. As I loved and honoured her, " said Wilding, reverently kissing his hand towards the picture, and then covering his eyes with it. "As I loved and honoured her, and have a world of reasons to be grateful to her! " And so broke down again.

His partner rose from the chair he had occupied, and stood beside him with a hand softly laid upon his shoulder. "Walter, I knew you before to- day to be an upright man, with a pure conscience and a fine heart. It is very fortunate for me that I have the privilege to travel on in life so near to so trustworthy a man. I am thankful for it. Use me as your right hand, and rely upon me to the death. Don't think the worse of me if I protest to you that my uppermost feeling at present is a confused, you may call it an unreasonable, one. I feel far more pity for the lady and for you, because you did not stand in your supposed relations, than I can feel for the unknown man (if he ever became a man), because he was unconsciously displaced. You have done well in sending for Mr. Bintrey. What I think will be a part of his advice, I know is the whole of mine. Do not move a step in this serious matter precipitately. The secret must be kept among us with great strictness, for to part with it lightly would be to invite fraudulent claims, to encourage a host of knaves, to let loose a flood of perjury and plotting. I have no more to say now, Walter, than to remind you that you sold me a share in your business, expressly to save yourself from more work than your present health is fit for, and that I bought it expressly to do work, and mean to do it. "

With these words, and a parting grip of his partner's shoulder that gave them the best emphasis they could have had, George Vendale betook himself presently to the counting-house, and presently afterwards to the address of M. Jules Obenreizer.

As he turned into Soho Square, and directed his steps towards its north side, a deepened colour shot across his sun-browned face, which Wilding, if he had been a better observer, or had been less occupied with his own trouble, might have noticed when his partner read aloud a certain passage in their Swiss correspondent's letter, which he had not read so distinctly as the rest.

A curious colony of mountaineers has long been enclosed within that small flat London district of Soho. Swiss watchmakers, Swiss silver-chasers, Swiss jewellers, Swiss importers of Swiss musical boxes and Swiss toys of various kinds, draw close together there. Swiss professors of music, painting, and languages; Swiss artificers in steady work; Swiss couriers, and other Swiss servants chronically out of place; industrious Swiss laundresses and clear-starchers; mysteriously existing Swiss of both sexes; Swiss creditable and Swiss discreditable; Swiss to be trusted by all means, and Swiss to be trusted by no means; these diverse Swiss particles are attracted to a centre in the district of Soho. Shabby Swiss eating-houses, coffee-houses, and lodging-houses, Swiss drinks and dishes, Swiss service for Sundays, and Swiss schools for week-days, are all to be found there. Even the native-born English taverns drive a sort of broken-English trade; announcing in their windows Swiss whets and drams, and sheltering in their bars Swiss skirmishes of love and animosity on most nights in the year.

When the new partner in Wilding and Co. rang the bell of a door bearing the blunt inscription OBENREIZER on a brass plate—the inner door of a substantial house, whose ground story was devoted to the sale of Swiss clocks—he passed at once into domestic Switzerland. A white-tiled stove for winter-time filled the fireplace of the room into which he was shown, the room's bare floor was laid together in a neat pattern of several ordinary woods, the room had a prevalent air of surface bareness and much scrubbing; and the little square of flowery carpet by the sofa, and the velvet chimney-board with its capacious clock and vases of artificial flowers, contended with that tone, as if, in bringing out the whole effect, a Parisian had adapted a dairy to domestic purposes.

Mimic water was dropping off a mill-wheel under the clock. The visitor had not stood before it, following it with his eyes, a minute, when M. Obenreizer, at his elbow, startled him by saying, in very good English, very slightly clipped: "How do you do? So glad! "

"I beg your pardon. I didn't hear you come in. "

"Not at all! Sit, please. "

Releasing his visitor's two arms, which he had lightly pinioned at the elbows by way of embrace, M. Obenreizer also sat, remarking, with a smile: "You are well? So glad! " and touching his elbows again.

"I don't know, " said Vendale, after exchange of salutations, "whether you may yet have heard of me from your House at Neuchatel? "

"Ah, yes! "

"In connection with Wilding and Co.? "

"Ah, surely! "

"Is it not odd that I should come to you, in London here, as one of the Firm of Wilding and Co., to pay the Firm's respects? "

"Not at all! What did I always observe when we were on the mountains? We call them vast; but the world is so little. So little is the world, that one cannot keep away from persons. There are so few persons in the world, that they continually cross and re-cross. So very little is the world, that one cannot get rid of a person. Not, " touching his elbows again, with an ingratiatory smile, "that one would desire to get rid of you. "

"I hope not, M. Obenreizer. "

"Please call me, in your country, Mr. I call myself so, for I love your country. If I *could* be English! But I am born. And you? Though descended from so fine a family, you have had the condescension to come into trade? Stop though. Wines? Is it trade in England or profession? Not fine art? "

"Mr. Obenreizer, " returned Vendale, somewhat out of countenance, "I was but a silly young fellow, just of age, when I first had the pleasure of travelling with you, and when you and I and Mademoiselle your niece—who is well? "

"Thank you. Who is well. "

"—Shared some slight glacier dangers together. If, with a boy's vanity, I rather vaunted my family, I hope I did so as a kind of introduction of myself. It was very weak, and in very bad taste; but perhaps you know our English proverb, 'Live and Learn.'"

"You make too much of it, " returned the Swiss. "And what the devil! After all, yours *was* a fine family. "

George Vendale's laugh betrayed a little vexation as he rejoined: "Well! I was strongly attached to my parents, and when we first travelled together, Mr. Obenreizer, I was in the first flush of coming into what my father and mother left me. So I hope it may have been, after all, more youthful openness of speech and heart than boastfulness. "

"All openness of speech and heart! No boastfulness! " cried Obenreizer. "You tax yourself too heavily. You tax yourself, my faith! as if you was your Government taxing you! Besides, it commenced with me. I remember, that evening in the boat upon the lake, floating among the reflections of the mountains and valleys, the crags and pine woods, which were my earliest remembrance, I drew a word-picture of my sordid childhood. Of our poor hut, by the waterfall which my mother showed to travellers; of the cow-shed where I slept with the cow; of my idiot half-brother always sitting at the door, or limping down the Pass to beg; of my half-sister always spinning, and resting her enormous goitre on a great stone; of my being a famished naked little wretch of two or three years, when they were men and women with hard hands to beat me, I, the only child of my father's second marriage—if it even was a marriage. What more natural than for you to compare notes with me, and say,

'We are as one by age; at that same time I sat upon my mother's lap in my father's carriage, rolling through the rich English streets, all luxury surrounding me, all squalid poverty kept far from me. Such is *my* earliest remembrance as opposed to yours! '"

Mr. Obenreizer was a black-haired young man of a dark complexion, through whose swarthy skin no red glow ever shone. When colour would have come into another cheek, a hardly discernible beat would come into his, as if the machinery for bringing up the ardent blood were there, but the machinery were dry. He was robustly made, well proportioned, and had handsome features. Many would have perceived that some surface change in him would have set them more at their ease with him, without being able to define what change. If his lips could have been made much thicker, and his neck much thinner, they would have found their want supplied.

But the great Obenreizer peculiarity was, that a certain nameless film would come over his eyes—apparently by the action of his own will—which would impenetrably veil, not only from those tellers of tales, but from his face at large, every expression save one of attention. It by no means followed that his attention should be wholly given to the person with whom he spoke, or even wholly bestowed on present sounds and objects. Rather, it was a comprehensive watchfulness of everything he had in his own mind, and everything that he knew to be, or suspected to be, in the minds of other men.

At this stage of the conversation, Mr. Obenreizer's film came over him.

"The object of my present visit, " said Vendale, "is, I need hardly say, to assure you of the friendliness of Wilding and Co., and of the goodness of your credit with us, and of our desire to be of service to you. We hope shortly to offer you our hospitality. Things are not quite in train with us yet, for my partner, Mr. Wilding, is reorganising the domestic part of our establishment, and is interrupted by some private affairs. You don't know Mr. Wilding, I believe? "

Mr. Obenreizer did not.

"You must come together soon. He will be glad to have made your acquaintance, and I think I may predict that you will be glad to have made his. You have not been long established in London, I suppose, Mr. Obenreizer? "

"It is only now that I have undertaken this agency. "

"Mademoiselle your niece — is — not married? "

"Not married. "

George Vendale glanced about him, as if for any tokens of her.

"She has been in London? "

"She *is* in London. "

"When, and where, might I have the honour of recalling myself to her remembrance? "

Mr. Obenreizer, discarding his film and touching his visitor's elbows as before, said lightly: "Come up-stairs. "

Fluttered enough by the suddenness with which the interview he had sought was coming upon him after all, George Vendale followed up-stairs. In a room over the chamber he had just quitted — a room also Swiss-appointed — a young lady sat near one of three windows, working at an embroidery-frame; and an older lady sat with her face turned close to another white-tiled stove (though it was summer, and the stove was not lighted), cleaning gloves. The young lady wore an unusual quantity of fair bright hair, very prettily braided about a rather rounder white forehead than the average English type, and so her face might have been a shade — or say a light — rounder than the average English face, and her figure slightly rounder than the figure of the average English girl at nineteen. A remarkable indication of freedom and grace of limb, in her quiet attitude, and a wonderful purity and freshness of colour in her dimpled face and bright gray eyes, seemed fraught with mountain air. Switzerland too, though the general fashion of her dress was English, peeped out of the fanciful bodice she wore, and lurked in the curious clocked red stocking, and in its little silver-buckled shoe. As to the elder lady, sitting with her feet apart upon the lower brass ledge of the stove, supporting a lap-full of gloves while she cleaned one stretched on her left hand, she was a true Swiss impersonation of another kind; from the breadth of her cushion-like back, and the ponderosity of her respectable legs (if the word be admissible), to the black velvet band tied tightly round her throat for the repression of a rising tendency to goitre; or, higher still, to her great copper-coloured gold ear-rings; or, higher still, to her head-dress of black gauze stretched on wire.

"Miss Marguerite, " said Obenreizer to the young lady, "do you recollect this gentleman? "

"I think, " she answered, rising from her seat, surprised and a little confused: "it is Mr. Vendale? "

"I think it is, " said Obenreizer, dryly. "Permit me, Mr. Vendale. Madame Dor. "

The elder lady by the stove, with the glove stretched on her left hand, like a glover's sign, half got up, half looked over her broad shoulder, and wholly plumped down again and rubbed away.

"Madame Dor, " said Obenreizer, smiling, "is so kind as to keep me free from stain or tear. Madame Dor humours my weakness for being always neat, and devotes her time to removing every one of my specks and spots. "

Madame Dor, with the stretched glove in the air, and her eyes closely scrutinizing its palm, discovered a tough spot in Mr. Obenreizer at that instant, and rubbed hard at him. George Vendale took his seat by the embroidery-frame (having first taken the fair right hand that his entrance had checked), and glanced at the gold cross that dipped into the bodice, with something of the devotion of a pilgrim who had reached his shrine at last. Obenreizer stood in the middle of the room with his thumbs in his waistcoat-pockets, and became filmy.

"He was saying down-stairs, Miss Obenreizer, " observed Vendale, "that the world is so small a place, that people cannot escape one another. I have found it much too large for me since I saw you last. "

"Have you travelled so far, then? " she inquired.

"Not so far, for I have only gone back to Switzerland each year; but I could have wished—and indeed I have wished very often—that the little world did not afford such opportunities for long escapes as it does. If it had been less, I might have found my follow-travellers sooner, you know. "

The pretty Marguerite coloured, and very slightly glanced in the direction of Madame Dor.

"You find us at length, Mr. Vendale. Perhaps you may lose us again. "

"I trust not. The curious coincidence that has enabled me to find you, encourages me to hope not. "

"What is that coincidence, sir, if you please? " A dainty little native touch in this turn of speech, and in its tone, made it perfectly captivating, thought George Vendale, when again he noticed an instantaneous glance towards Madame Dor. A caution seemed to be conveyed in it, rapid flash though it was; so he quietly took heed of Madame Dor from that time forth.

"It is that I happen to have become a partner in a House of business in London, to which Mr. Obenreizer happens this very day to be expressly recommended: and that, too, by another house of business in Switzerland, in which (as it turns out) we both have a commercial interest. He has not told you? "

"Ah! " cried Obenreizer, striking in, filmless. "No. I had not told Miss Marguerite. The world is so small and so monotonous that a surprise is worth having in such a little jog-trot place. It is as he tells you, Miss Marguerite. He, of so fine a family, and so proudly bred, has condescended to trade. To trade! Like us poor peasants who have risen from ditches! "

A cloud crept over the fair brow, and she cast down her eyes.

"Why, it is good for trade! " pursued Obenreizer, enthusiastically. "It ennobles trade! It is the misfortune of trade, it is its vulgarity, that any low people—for example, we poor peasants—may take to it and climb by it. See you, my dear Vendale! " He spoke with great energy. "The father of Miss Marguerite, my eldest half-brother, more than two times your age or mine, if living now, wandered without shoes, almost without rags, from that wretched Pass—wandered—wandered—got to be fed with the mules and dogs at an Inn in the main valley far away—got to be Boy there—got to be Ostler—got to be Waiter—got to be Cook—got to be Landlord. As Landlord, he

37

took me (could he take the idiot beggar his brother, or the spinning monstrosity his sister? ) to put as pupil to the famous watchmaker, his neighbour and friend. His wife dies when Miss Marguerite is born. What is his will, and what are his words to me, when he dies, she being between girl and woman? 'All for Marguerite, except so much by the year for you. You are young, but I make her your ward, for you were of the obscurest and the poorest peasantry, and so was I, and so was her mother; we were abject peasants all, and you will remember it. ' The thing is equally true of most of my countrymen, now in trade in this your London quarter of Soho. Peasants once; low-born drudging Swiss Peasants. Then how good and great for trade: " here, from having been warm, he became playfully jubilant, and touched the young wine-merchant's elbows again with his light embrace: "to be exalted by gentlemen. "

"I do not think so, " said Marguerite, with a flushed cheek, and a look away from the visitor, that was almost defiant. "I think it is as much exalted by us peasants. "

"Fie, fie, Miss Marguerite, " said Obenreizer. "You speak in proud England. "

"I speak in proud earnest, " she answered, quietly resuming her work, "and I am not English, but a Swiss peasant's daughter. "

There was a dismissal of the subject in her words, which Vendale could not contend against. He only said in an earnest manner, "I most heartily agree with you, Miss Obenreizer, and I have already said so, as Mr. Obenreizer will bear witness, " which he by no means did, "in this house. "

Now, Vendale's eyes were quick eyes, and sharply watching Madame Dor by times, noted something in the broad back view of that lady. There was considerable pantomimic expression in her glove-cleaning. It had been very softly done when he spoke with Marguerite, or it had altogether stopped, like the action of a listener. When Obenreizer's peasant-speech came to an end, she rubbed most vigorously, as if applauding it. And once or twice, as the glove (which she always held before her a little above her face) turned in the air, or as this finger went down, or that went up, he even fancied that it made some telegraphic communication to Obenreizer: whose back was certainly never turned upon it, though he did not seem at all to heed it.

38

Vendale observed too, that in Marguerite's dismissal of the subject twice forced upon him to his misrepresentation, there was an indignant treatment of her guardian which she tried to cheek: as though she would have flamed out against him, but for the influence of fear. He also observed — though this was not much — that he never advanced within the distance of her at which he first placed himself: as though there were limits fixed between them. Neither had he ever spoken of her without the prefix "Miss, " though whenever he uttered it, it was with the faintest trace of an air of mockery. And now it occurred to Vendale for the first time that something curious in the man, which he had never before been able to define, was definable as a certain subtle essence of mockery that eluded touch or analysis. He felt convinced that Marguerite was in some sort a prisoner as to her freewill — though she held her own against those two combined, by the force of her character, which was nevertheless inadequate to her release. To feel convinced of this, was not to feel less disposed to love her than he had always been. In a word, he was desperately in love with her, and thoroughly determined to pursue the opportunity which had opened at last.

For the present, he merely touched upon the pleasure that Wilding and Co. would soon have in entreating Miss Obenreizer to honour their establishment with her presence — a curious old place, though a bachelor house withal — and so did not protract his visit beyond such a visit's ordinary length. Going down-stairs, conducted by his host, he found the Obenreizer counting-house at the back of the entrance-hall, and several shabby men in outlandish garments hanging about, whom Obenreizer put aside that he might pass, with a few words in *patois*.

"Countrymen, " he explained, as he attended Vendale to the door. "Poor compatriots. Grateful and attached, like dogs! Good-bye. To meet again. So glad! "

Two more light touches on his elbows dismissed him into the street.

Sweet Marguerite at her frame, and Madame Dor's broad back at her telegraph, floated before him to Cripple Corner. On his arrival there, Wilding was closeted with Bintrey. The cellar doors happening to be open, Vendale lighted a candle in a cleft stick, and went down for a cellarous stroll. Graceful Marguerite floated before him faithfully, but Madame Dor's broad back remained outside.

The vaults were very spacious, and very old. There had been a stone crypt down there, when bygones were not bygones; some said, part of a monkish refectory; some said, of a chapel; some said, of a Pagan temple. It was all one now. Let who would make what he liked of a crumbled pillar and a broken arch or so. Old Time had made what *he* liked of it, and was quite indifferent to contradiction.

The close air, the musty smell, and the thunderous rumbling in the streets above, as being, out of the routine of ordinary life, went well enough with the picture of pretty Marguerite holding her own against those two. So Vendale went on until, at a turning in the vaults, he saw a light like the light he carried.

"O! You are here, are you, Joey? "

"Oughtn't it rather to go, 'O! *You're* here, are you, Master George? ' For it's my business to be here. But it ain't yourn. "

"Don't grumble, Joey. "

"O! *I* don't grumble, " returned the Cellarman. "If anything grumbles, it's what I've took in through the pores; it ain't me. Have a care as something in you don't begin a grumbling, Master George. Stop here long enough for the wapours to work, and they'll be at it. "

His present occupation consisted of poking his head into the bins, making measurements and mental calculations, and entering them in a rhinoceros- hide-looking note-book, like a piece of himself.

"They'll be at it, " he resumed, laying the wooden rod that he measured with across two casks, entering his last calculation, and straightening his back, "trust 'em! And so you've regularly come into the business, Master George? "

"Regularly. I hope you don't object, Joey? "

"*I* don't, bless you. But Wapours objects that you're too young. You're both on you too young. "

"We shall got over that objection day by day, Joey. "

"Ay, Master George; but I shall day by day get over the objection that I'm too old, and so I shan't be capable of seeing much improvement in you. "

The retort so tickled Joey Ladle that he grunted forth a laugh and delivered it again, grunting forth another laugh after the second edition of "improvement in you. "

"But what's no laughing matter, Master George, " he resumed, straightening his back once more, "is, that young Master Wilding has gone and changed the luck. Mark my words. He has changed the luck, and he'll find it out. I ain't been down here all my life for nothing! I know by what I notices down here, when it's a-going to rain, when it's a-going to hold up, when it's a-going to blow, when it's a-going to be calm. I know, by what I notices down here, when the luck's changed, quite as well. "

"Has this growth on the roof anything to do with your divination? " asked Vendale, holding his light towards a gloomy ragged growth of dark fungus, pendent from the arches with a very disagreeable and repellent effect. "We are famous for this growth in this vault, aren't we? "

"We are Master George, " replied Joey Ladle, moving a step or two away, "and if you'll be advised by me, you'll let it alone. "

Taking up the rod just now laid across the two casks, and faintly moving the languid fungus with it, Vendale asked, "Ay, indeed? Why so? "

"Why, not so much because it rises from the casks of wine, and may leave you to judge what sort of stuff a Cellarman takes into himself when he walks in the same all the days of his life, nor yet so much because at a stage of its growth it's maggots, and you'll fetch 'em down upon you, " returned Joey Ladle, still keeping away, "as for another reason, Master George. "

"What other reason? "

"(I wouldn't keep on touchin' it, if I was you, sir. ) I'll tell you if you'll come out of the place. First, take a look at its colour, Master George. "

"I am doing so. "

"Done, sir. Now, come out of the place. "

He moved away with his light, and Vendale followed with his. When Vendale came up with him, and they were going back together, Vendale, eyeing him as they walked through the arches, said: "Well, Joey? The colour. "

"Is it like clotted blood, Master George? "

"Like enough, perhaps. "

"More than enough, I think, " muttered Joey Ladle, shaking his head solemnly.

"Well, say it is like; say it is exactly like. What then? "

"Master George, they do say—"

"Who? "

"How should I know who? " rejoined the Cellarman, apparently much exasperated by the unreasonable nature of the question. "Them! Them as says pretty well everything, you know. How should I know who They are, if you don't? "

"True. Go on. "

"They do say that the man that gets by any accident a piece of that dark growth right upon his breast, will, for sure and certain, die by murder. "

As Vendale laughingly stopped to meet the Cellarman's eyes, which he had fastened on his light while dreamily saying those words, he suddenly became conscious of being struck upon his own breast by a heavy hand. Instantly following with his eyes the action of the hand that struck him—which was his companion's—he saw that it had beaten off his breast a web or clot of the fungus even then floating to the ground.

For a moment he turned upon the Cellarman almost as scared a look as the Cellarman turned upon him. But in another moment they had reached the daylight at the foot of the cellar-steps, and before he cheerfully sprang up them, he blew out his candle and the superstition together.

## EXIT WILDING

On the morning of the next day, Wilding went out alone, after leaving a message with his clerk. "If Mr. Vendale should ask for me, " he said, "or if Mr. Bintrey should call, tell them I am gone to the Foundling. " All that his partner had said to him, all that his lawyer, following on the same side, could urge, had left him persisting unshaken in his own point of view. To find the lost man, whose place he had usurped, was now the paramount interest of his life, and to inquire at the Foundling was plainly to take the first step in the direction of discovery. To the Foundling, accordingly, the wine-merchant now went.

The once familiar aspect of the building was altered to him, as the look of the portrait over the chimney-piece was altered to him. His one dearest association with the place which had sheltered his childhood had been broken away from it for ever. A strange reluctance possessed him, when he stated his business at the door. His heart ached as he sat alone in the waiting-room while the Treasurer of the institution was being sent for to see him. When the interview began, it was only by a painful effort that he could compose himself sufficiently to mention the nature of his errand.

The Treasurer listened with a face which promised all needful attention, and promised nothing more.

"We are obliged to be cautious, " he said, when it came to his turn to speak, "about all inquiries which are made by strangers. "

"You can hardly consider me a stranger, " answered Wilding, simply. "I was one of your poor lost children here, in the bygone time. "

The Treasurer politely rejoined that this circumstance inspired him with a special interest in his visitor. But he pressed, nevertheless for that visitor's motive in making his inquiry. Without further preface, Wilding told him his motive, suppressing nothing. The Treasurer rose, and led the way into the room in which the registers of the institution were kept. "All the information which our books can give is heartily at your service, " he said. "After the time that has elapsed, I am afraid it is the only information we have to offer you. "

The books were consulted, and the entry was found expressed as follows:

"3d March, 1836. Adopted, and removed from the Foundling Hospital, a male infant, named Walter Wilding. Name and condition of the person adopting the child—Mrs. Jane Ann Miller, widow. Address—Lime-Tree Lodge, Groombridge Wells. References—the Reverend John Harker, Groombridge Wells; and Messrs. Giles, Jeremie, and Giles, bankers, Lombard Street. "

"Is that all? " asked the wine-merchant. "Had you no after-communication with Mrs. Miller? "

"None—or some reference to it must have appeared in this book. "

"May I take a copy of the entry? "

"Certainly! You are a little agitated. Let me make a copy for you. "

"My only chance, I suppose, " said Wilding, looking sadly at the copy, "is to inquire at Mrs. Miller's residence, and to try if her references can help me? "

"That is the only chance I see at present, " answered the Treasurer. "I heartily wish I could have been of some further assistance to you. "

With those farewell words to comfort him Wilding set forth on the journey of investigation which began from the Foundling doors. The first stage to make for, was plainly the house of business of the bankers in Lombard Street. Two of the partners in the firm were inaccessible to chance-visitors when he asked for them. The third, after raising certain inevitable difficulties, consented to let a clerk examine the ledger marked with the initial letter "M. " The account of Mrs. Miller, widow, of Groombridge Wells, was found. Two long lines, in faded ink, were drawn across it; and at the bottom of the page there appeared this note: "Account closed, September 30th, 1837. "

So the first stage of the journey was reached—and so it ended in No Thoroughfare! After sending a note to Cripple Corner to inform his partner that his absence might be prolonged for some hours, Wilding took his place in the train, and started for the second stage on the journey—Mrs. Miller's residence at Groombridge Wells.

Mothers and children travelled with him; mothers and children met each other at the station; mothers and children were in the shops when he entered them to inquire for Lime-Tree Lodge. Everywhere, the nearest and dearest of human relations showed itself happily in the happy light of day. Everywhere, he was reminded of the treasured delusion from which he had been awakened so cruelly—of the lost memory which had passed from him like a reflection from a glass.

Inquiring here, inquiring there, he could hear of no such place as Lime- Tree Lodge. Passing a house-agent's office, he went in wearily, and put the question for the last time. The house-agent pointed across the street to a dreary mansion of many windows, which might have been a manufactory, but which was an hotel. "That's where Lime-Tree Lodge stood, sir, " said the man, "ten years ago. "

The second stage reached, and No Thoroughfare again!

But one chance was left. The clerical reference, Mr. Harker, still remained to be found. Customers coming in at the moment to occupy the house-agent's attention, Wilding went down the street, and entering a bookseller's shop, asked if he could be informed of the Reverend John Harker's present address.

The bookseller looked unaffectedly shocked and astonished, and made no answer.

Wilding repeated his question.

The bookseller took up from his counter a prim little volume in a binding of sober gray. He handed it to his visitor, open at the title-page. Wilding read:

"The martyrdom of the Reverend John Harker in New Zealand. Related by a former member of his flock. "

Wilding put the book down on the counter. "I beg your pardon, " he said thinking a little, perhaps, of his own present martyrdom while he spoke. The silent bookseller acknowledged the apology by a bow. Wilding went out.

Third and last stage, and No Thoroughfare for the third and last time.

There was nothing more to be done; there was absolutely no choice but to go back to London, defeated at all points. From time to time on the return journey, the wine-merchant looked at his copy of the entry in the Foundling Register. There is one among the many forms of despair—perhaps the most pitiable of all—which persists in disguising itself as Hope. Wilding checked himself in the act of throwing the useless morsel of paper out of the carriage window. "It may lead to something yet, " he thought. "While I live, I won't part with it. When I die, my executors shall find it sealed up with my will. "

Now, the mention of his will set the good wine-merchant on a new track of thought, without diverting his mind from its engrossing subject. He must make his will immediately.

The application of the phrase No Thoroughfare to the case had originated with Mr. Bintrey. In their first long conference following the discovery, that sagacious personage had a hundred times repeated, with an obstructive shake of the head, "No Thoroughfare, Sir, No Thoroughfare. My belief is that there is no way out of this at this time of day, and my advice is, make yourself comfortable where you are. "

In the course of the protracted consultation, a magnum of the forty-five year old port-wine had been produced for the wetting of Mr. Bintrey's legal whistle; but the more clearly he saw his way through the wine, the more emphatically he did not see his way through the case; repeating as often as he set his glass down empty. "Mr. Wilding, No Thoroughfare. Rest and be thankful. "

It is certain that the honest wine-merchant's anxiety to make a will originated in profound conscientiousness; though it is possible (and quite consistent with his rectitude) that he may unconsciously have derived some feeling of relief from the prospect of delegating his own difficulty to two other men who were to come after him. Be that as it may, he pursued his new track of thought with great ardour, and lost no time in begging George Vendale and Mr. Bintrey to meet him in Cripple Corner and share his confidence.

"Being all three assembled with closed doors, " said Mr. Bintrey, addressing the new partner on the occasion, "I wish to observe, before our friend (and my client) entrusts us with his further views, that I have endorsed what I understand from him to have been your advice, Mr. Vendale, and what would be the advice of every sensible man. I have told him that he positively must keep his secret. I have spoken with Mrs. Goldstraw, both in his presence and in his absence; and if anybody is to be trusted (which is a very large IF), I think she is to be trusted to that extent. I have pointed out to our friend (and my client), that to set on foot random inquiries would not only be to raise the Devil, in the likeness of all the swindlers in the kingdom, but would also be to waste the estate. Now, you see, Mr. Vendale, our friend (and my client) does not desire to waste the estate, but, on the contrary, desires to husband it for what he considers—but I can't say I do—the rightful owner, if such rightful owner should ever be found. I am very much mistaken if he ever will be, but never mind that. Mr. Wilding and I are, at least, agreed that the estate is not to be wasted. Now, I have yielded to Mr. Wilding's desire to keep an advertisement at intervals flowing through the newspapers, cautiously inviting any person who may know anything about that adopted infant, taken from the Foundling Hospital, to come to my office; and I have pledged myself that such advertisement shall regularly appear. I have gathered from our friend (and my client) that I meet you here to-day to take his instructions, not to give him advice. I am prepared to receive his instructions, and to respect his wishes; but you will please observe that this does not imply my approval of either as a matter of professional opinion. "

Thus Mr. Bintrey; talking quite is much *at* Wilding as *to* Vendale. And yet, in spite of his care for his client, he was so amused by his client's Quixotic conduct, as to eye him from time to time with twinkling eyes, in the light of a highly comical curiosity.

"Nothing, " observed Wilding, "can be clearer. I only wish my head were as clear as yours, Mr. Bintrey. "

"If you feel that singing in it coming on, " hinted the lawyer, with an alarmed glance, "put it off. —I mean the interview. "

"Not at all, I thank you, " said Wilding. "What was I going to—"

"Don't excite yourself, Mr. Wilding, " urged the lawyer.

"No; I *wasn't* going to, " said the wine-merchant. "Mr. Bintrey and George Vendale, would you have any hesitation or objection to become my joint trustees and executors, or can you at once consent? "

"*I* consent, " replied George Vendale, readily.

"*I* consent, " said Bintrey, not so readily.

"Thank you both. Mr. Bintrey, my instructions for my last will and testament are short and plain. Perhaps you will now have the goodness to take them down. I leave the whole of my real and personal estate, without any exception or reservation whatsoever, to you two, my joint trustees and executors, in trust to pay over the whole to the true Walter Wilding, if he shall be found and identified within two years after the day of my death. Failing that, in trust to you two to pay over the whole as a benefaction and legacy to the Foundling Hospital. "

"Those are all your instructions, are they, Mr. Wilding? " demanded Bintrey, after a blank silence, during which nobody had looked at anybody.

"The whole. "

"And as to those instructions, you have absolutely made up your mind, Mr. Wilding? "

"Absolutely, decidedly, finally. "

"It only remains, " said the lawyer, with one shrug of his shoulders, "to get them into technical and binding form, and to execute and attest. Now, does that press? Is there any hurry about it? You are not going to die yet, sir. "

"Mr. Bintrey, " answered Wilding, gravely, "when I am going to die is within other knowledge than yours or mine. I shall be glad to have this matter off my mind, if you please. "

"We are lawyer and client again, " rejoined Bintrey, who, for the nonce, had become almost sympathetic. "If this day week—here, at the same hour—will suit Mr. Vendale and yourself, I will enter in my Diary that I attend you accordingly. "

The appointment was made, and in due sequence, kept. The will was formally signed, sealed, delivered, and witnessed, and was carried off by Mr. Bintrey for safe storage among the papers of his clients, ranged in their respective iron boxes, with their respective owners' names outside, on iron tiers in his consulting-room, as if that legal sanctuary were a condensed Family Vault of Clients.

With more heart than he had lately had for former subjects of interest, Wilding then set about completing his patriarchal establishment, being much assisted not only by Mrs. Goldstraw but by Vendale too: who, perhaps, had in his mind the giving of an Obenreizer dinner as soon as possible. Anyhow, the establishment being reported in sound working order, the Obenreizers, Guardian and Ward, were asked to dinner, and Madame Dor was included in the invitation. If Vendale had been over head and ears in love before—a phrase not to be taken as implying the faintest doubt about it—this dinner plunged him down in love ten thousand fathoms deep. Yet, for the life of him, he could not get one word alone with charming Marguerite. So surely as a blessed moment seemed to come, Obenreizer, in his filmy state, would stand at Vendale's elbow, or the broad back of Madame Dor would appear before his eyes. That speechless matron was never seen in a front view, from the moment of her arrival to that of her departure—except at dinner. And from the instant of her retirement to the drawing-room, after a hearty participation in that meal, she turned her face to the wall again.

Yet, through four or five delightful though distracting hours, Marguerite was to be seen, Marguerite was to be heard, Marguerite was to be occasionally touched. When they made the round of the old dark cellars, Vendale led her by the hand; when she sang to him in the lighted room at night, Vendale, standing by her, held her relinquished gloves, and would have bartered against them every drop of the forty-five year old, though it had been forty-five times forty-five years old, and its nett price forty-five times forty-five pounds per dozen. And still, when she was gone, and a great gap of an extinguisher was clapped on Cripple Corner, he tormented himself by wondering, Did she think that he admired her! Did she think that he adored her! Did she suspect that she had won him, heart and soul! Did she care to think at all about it! And so, Did she and Didn't she, up and down the gamut, and above the line and below the line, dear, dear! Poor restless heart of humanity! To think that the men who were mummies thousands of years ago, did the same, and ever found the secret how to be quiet after it!

"What do you think, George, " Wilding asked him next day, "of Mr. Obenreizer? (I won't ask you what you think of Miss Obenreizer. )"

"I don't know, " said Vendale, "and I never did know, what to think of him. "

"He is well informed and clever, " said Wilding.

"Certainly clever. "

"A good musician. " (He had played very well, and sung very well, overnight. )

"Unquestionably a good musician. "

"And talks well. "

"Yes, " said George Vendale, ruminating, "and talks well. Do you know, Wilding, it oddly occurs to me, as I think about him, that he doesn't keep silence well! "

"How do you mean? He is not obtrusively talkative. "

"No, and I don't mean that. But when he is silent, you can hardly help vaguely, though perhaps most unjustly, mistrusting him. Take people whom you know and like. Take any one you know and like. "

"Soon done, my good fellow, " said Wilding. "I take you. "

"I didn't bargain for that, or foresee it, " returned Vendale, laughing. "However, take me. Reflect for a moment. Is your approving knowledge of my interesting face mainly founded (however various the momentary expressions it may include) on my face when I am silent? "

"I think it is, " said Wilding.

"I think so too. Now, you see, when Obenreizer speaks—in other words, when he is allowed to explain himself away—he comes out right enough; but when he has not the opportunity of explaining himself away, he comes out rather wrong. Therefore it is, that I say he does not keep silence well. And passing hastily in review such faces as I know, and don't trust, I am inclined to think, now I give my mind to it, that none of them keep silence well. "

This proposition in Physiognomy being new to Wilding, he was at first slow to admit it, until asking himself the question whether Mrs. Goldstraw kept silence well, and remembering that her face in repose decidedly invited trustfulness, he was as glad as men usually are to believe what they desire to believe.

But, as he was very slow to regain his spirits or his health, his partner, as another means of setting him up—and perhaps also with contingent Obenreizer views—reminded him of those musical schemes of his in connection with his family, and how a singing-class was to be formed in the house, and a Choir in a neighbouring church. The class was established speedily, and, two or three of the people having already some musical knowledge, and singing tolerably, the Choir soon followed. The latter was led, and chiefly taught, by Wilding himself: who had hopes of converting his dependents into so many Foundlings, in respect of their capacity to sing sacred choruses.

Now, the Obenreizers being skilled musicians, it was easily brought to pass that they should be asked to join these musical unions. Guardian and Ward consenting, or Guardian consenting for both, it was necessarily brought to pass that Vendale's life became a life of absolute thraldom and enchantment. For, in the mouldy Christopher-Wren church on Sundays, with its dearly beloved brethren assembled and met together, five-and- twenty strong, was not that Her voice that shot like light into the darkest places, thrilling the walls and pillars as though they were pieces of his heart! What time, too, Madame Dor in a corner of the high pew, turning her back upon everybody and everything, could not fail to be Ritualistically right at some moment of the service; like the man whom the doctors recommended to get drunk once a month, and who, that he might not overlook it, got drunk every day.

But, even those seraphic Sundays were surpassed by the Wednesday concerts established for the patriarchal family. At those concerts she would sit down to the piano and sing them, in her own tongue, songs of her own land, songs calling from the mountain-tops to Vendale, "Rise above the grovelling level country; come far away from the crowd; pursue me as I mount higher; higher, higher, melting into the azure distance; rise to my supremest height of all, and love me here! " Then would the pretty bodice, the clocked stocking, and the silver-buckled shoe be, like the broad forehead and the bright eyes, fraught with the spring of a very chamois, until the strain was over.

Not even over Vendale himself did these songs of hers cast a more potent spell than over Joey Ladle in his different way. Steadily refusing to muddle the harmony by taking any share in it, and evincing the supremest contempt for scales and such-like rudiments of music—which, indeed, seldom captivate mere listeners—Joey did at first give up the whole business for a bad job, and the whole of the performers for a set of howling Dervishes. But, descrying traces of unmuddled harmony in a part- song one day, he gave his two under cellarmen faint hopes of getting on towards something in course of time. An anthem of Handel's led to further encouragement from him: though he objected that that great musician must have been down in some of them foreign cellars pretty much, for to go and say the same thing so many times over; which, took it in how you might, he considered a certain sign of your having took it in somehow. On a third occasion, the public appearance of Mr. Jarvis with a flute, and of an odd man with a violin, and the performance of a duet by the two, did so astonish him that, solely of his own impulse and motion, he became inspired with the words, "Ann Koar! " repeatedly pronouncing them as if calling in a familiar manner for some lady who had distinguished herself in the orchestra. But this was his final testimony to the merits of his mates, for, the instrumental duet being performed at the first Wednesday concert, and being presently followed by the voice of Marguerite Obenreizer, he sat with his mouth wide open, entranced, until she had finished; when, rising in his place with much solemnity, and prefacing what he was about to say with a bow that specially included Mr. Wilding in it, he delivered himself of the gratifying sentiment: "Arter that, ye may all on ye get to bed! " And ever afterwards declined to render homage in any other words to the musical powers of the family.

Thus began a separate personal acquaintance between Marguerite Obenreizer and Joey Ladle. She laughed so heartily at his compliment, and yet was so abashed by it, that Joey made bold to say to her, after the concert was over, he hoped he wasn't so muddled in his head as to have took a liberty? She made him a gracious reply, and Joey ducked in return.

"You'll change the luck time about, Miss, " said Joey, ducking again. "It's such as you in the place that can bring round the luck of the place. "

"Can I? Round the luck? " she answered, in her pretty English, and with a pretty wonder. "I fear I do not understand. I am so stupid. "

"Young Master Wilding, Miss, " Joey explained confidentially, though not much to her enlightenment, "changed the luck, afore he took in young Master George. So I say, and so they'll find. Lord! Only come into the place and sing over the luck a few times, Miss, and it won't be able to help itself! "

With this, and with a whole brood of ducks, Joey backed out of the presence. But Joey being a privileged person, and even an involuntary conquest being pleasant to youth and beauty, Marguerite merrily looked out for him next time.

"Where is my Mr. Joey, please? " she asked Vendale.

So Joey was produced, and shaken hands with, and that became an Institution.

Another Institution arose in this wise. Joey was a little hard of hearing. He himself said it was "Wapours, " and perhaps it might have been; but whatever the cause of the effect, there the effect was, upon him. On this first occasion he had been seen to sidle along the wall, with his left hand to his left ear, until he had sidled himself into a seat pretty near the singer, in which place and position he had remained, until addressing to his friends the amateurs the compliment before mentioned. It was observed on the following Wednesday that Joey's action as a Pecking Machine was impaired at dinner, and it was rumoured about the table that this was explainable by his high-strung expectations of Miss Obenreizer's singing, and his fears of not getting a place where he could hear every note and syllable. The rumour reaching Wilding's ears, he in his good nature called Joey to the front at night before Marguerite began. Thus the Institution came into being that on succeeding nights, Marguerite, running her hands over the keys before singing, always said to Vendale, "Where is my Mr. Joey, please? " and that Vendale always brought him forth, and stationed him near by. That he should then, when all eyes were upon him, express in his face the utmost contempt for the exertions of his friends and confidence in Marguerite alone, whom he would stand contemplating, not unlike the rhinocerous out of the spelling- book, tamed and on his hind legs, was a part of the Institution. Also that when he remained after the singing in his most ecstatic state, some bold spirit from the back should say, "What do you think of it, Joey? " and he should be goaded to reply, as having that instant conceived the retort, "Arter that ye may all on ye get to bed! " These were other parts of the Institution.

But, the simple pleasures and small jests of Cripple Corner were not destined to have a long life. Underlying them from the first was a serious matter, which every member of the patriarchal family knew of, but which, by tacit agreement, all forbore to speak of. Mr. Wilding's health was in a bad way.

He might have overcome the shock he had sustained in the one great affection of his life, or he might have overcome his consciousness of being in the enjoyment of another man's property; but the two together were too much for him. A man haunted by twin ghosts, he became deeply depressed. The inseparable spectres sat at the board with him, ate from his platter, drank from his cup, and stood by his bedside at night. When he recalled his supposed mother's love, he felt as though he had stolen it. When he rallied a little under the respect and attachment of his dependants, he felt as though he were even fraudulent in making them happy, for that should have been the unknown man's duty and gratification.

Gradually, under the pressure of his brooding mind, his body stooped, his step lost its elasticity, his eyes were seldom lifted from the ground. He knew he could not help the deplorable mistake that had been made, but he knew he could not mend it; for the days and weeks went by, and no one claimed his name or his possessions. And now there began to creep over him a cloudy consciousness of often-recurring confusion in his head. He would unaccountably lose, sometimes whole hours, sometimes a whole day and night. Once, his remembrance stopped as he sat at the head of the dinner-table, and was blank until daybreak. Another time, it stopped as he was beating time to their singing, and went on again when he and his partner were walking in the court-yard by the light of the moon, half the night later. He asked Vendale (always full of consideration, work, and help) how this was? Vendale only replied, "You have not been quite well; that's all. " He looked for explanation into the faces of his people. But they would put it off with "Glad to see you looking so much better, sir; " or "Hope you're doing nicely now, sir; " in which was no information at all.

At length, when the partnership was but five months old, Walter Wilding took to his bed, and his housekeeper became his nurse.

"Lying here, perhaps you will not mind my calling you Sally, Mrs. Goldstraw? " said the poor wine-merchant.

"It sounds more natural to me, sir, than any other name, and I like it better. "

"Thank you, Sally. I think, Sally, I must of late have been subject to fits. Is that so, Sally? Don't mind telling me now. "

"It has happened, sir. "

"Ah! That is the explanation! " he quietly remarked. "Mr. Obenreizer, Sally, talks of the world being so small that it is not strange how often the same people come together, and come together at various places, and in various stages of life. But it does seem strange, Sally, that I should, as I may say, come round to the Foundling to die. "

He extended his hand to her, and she gently took it.

"You are not going to die, dear Mr. Wilding. "

"So Mr. Bintrey said, but I think he was wrong. The old child-feeling is coming back upon me, Sally. The old hush and rest, as I used to fall asleep. "

After an interval he said, in a placid voice, "Please kiss me, Nurse, " and, it was evident, believed himself to be lying in the old Dormitory.

As she had been used to bend over the fatherless and motherless children, Sally bent over the fatherless and motherless man, and put her lips to his forehead, murmuring:

"God bless you! "

"God bless you! " he replied, in the same tone.

After another interval, he opened his eyes in his own character, and said: "Don't move me, Sally, because of what I am going to say; I lie quite easily. I think my time is come, I don't know how it may appear to you, Sally, but—"

Insensibility fell upon him for a few minutes; he emerged from it once more.

"—I don't know how it may appear to you, Sally, but so it appears to me. "

When he had thus conscientiously finished his favourite sentence, his time came, and he died.

## ACT II.

## VENDALE MAKES LOVE

The summer and the autumn passed. Christmas and the New Year were at hand.

As executors honestly bent on performing their duty towards the dead, Vendale and Bintrey had held more than one anxious consultation on the subject of Wilding's will. The lawyer had declared, from the first, that it was simply impossible to take any useful action in the matter at all. The only obvious inquiries to make, in relation to the lost man, had been made already by Wilding himself; with this result, that time and death together had not left a trace of him discoverable. To advertise for the claimant to the property, it would be necessary to mention particulars—a course of proceeding which would invite half the impostors in England to present themselves in the character of the true Walter Wilding. "If we find a chance of tracing the lost man, we will take it. If we don't, let us meet for another consultation on the first anniversary of Wilding's death. " So Bintrey advised. And so, with the most earnest desire to fulfil his dead friend's wishes, Vendale was fain to let the matter rest for the present.

Turning from his interest in the past to his interest in the future, Vendale still found himself confronting a doubtful prospect. Months on months had passed since his first visit to Soho Square—and through all that time, the one language in which he had told Marguerite that he loved her was the language of the eyes, assisted, at convenient opportunities, by the language of the hand.

What was the obstacle in his way? The one immovable obstacle which had been in his way from the first. No matter how fairly the opportunities looked, Vendale's efforts to speak with Marguerite alone ended invariably in one and the same result. Under the most accidental circumstances, in the most innocent manner possible, Obenreizer was always in the way.

With the last days of the old year came an unexpected chance of spending an evening with Marguerite, which Vendale resolved should be a chance of speaking privately to her as well. A cordial note from Obenreizer invited him, on New Year's Day, to a little family dinner in Soho Square. "We shall be only four, " the note said. "We shall be only two, " Vendale determined, "before the evening is out! "

New Year's Day, among the English, is associated with the giving and receiving of dinners, and with nothing more. New Year's Day, among the foreigners, is the grand opportunity of the year for the giving and receiving of presents. It is occasionally possible to acclimatise a foreign custom. In this instance Vendale felt no hesitation about making the attempt. His one difficulty was to decide what his New Year's gift to Marguerite should be. The defensive pride of the peasant's daughter—morbidly sensitive to the inequality between her social position and his—would be secretly roused against him if he ventured on a rich offering. A gift, which a poor man's purse might purchase, was the one gift that could be trusted to find its way to her heart, for the giver's sake. Stoutly resisting temptation, in the form of diamonds and rubies, Vendale bought a brooch of the filagree-work of Genoa—the simplest and most unpretending ornament that he could find in the jeweller's shop.

He slipped his gift into Marguerite's hand as she held it out to welcome him on the day of the dinner.

"This is your first New Year's Day in England, " he said. "Will you let me help to make it like a New Year's Day at home? "

She thanked him, a little constrainedly, as she looked at the jeweller's box, uncertain what it might contain. Opening the box, and discovering the studiously simple form under which Vendale's little keepsake offered itself to her, she penetrated his motive on the spot. Her face turned on him brightly, with a look which said, "I own you have pleased and flattered me. " Never had she been so charming, in Vendale's eyes, as she was at that moment. Her winter dress—a petticoat of dark silk, with a bodice of black velvet rising to her neck, and enclosing it softly in a little circle of swansdown—heightened, by all the force of contrast, the dazzling fairness of her hair and her complexion. It was only when she turned aside from him to the glass, and, taking out the brooch that she wore, put his New Year's gift in its place, that Vendale's attention wandered far enough away from her to discover the presence of other persons in the room. He now became conscious that the hands of Obenreizer were affectionately in possession of his elbows. He now heard the voice of Obenreizer thanking him for his attention to Marguerite, with the

58

faintest possible ring of mockery in its tone. ("Such a simple present, dear sir! and showing such nice tact! ") He now discovered, for the first time, that there was one other guest, and but one, besides himself, whom Obenreizer presented as a compatriot and friend. The friend's face was mouldy, and the friend's figure was fat. His age was suggestive of the autumnal period of human life. In the course of the evening he developed two extraordinary capacities. One was a capacity for silence; the other was a capacity for emptying bottles.

Madame Dor was not in the room. Neither was there any visible place reserved for her when they sat down to table. Obenreizer explained that it was "the good Dor's simple habit to dine always in the middle of the day. She would make her excuses later in the evening. " Vendale wondered whether the good Dor had, on this occasion, varied her domestic employment from cleaning Obenreizer's gloves to cooking Obenreizer's dinner. This at least was certain—the dishes served were, one and all, as achievements in cookery, high above the reach of the rude elementary art of England. The dinner was unobtrusively perfect. As for the wine, the eyes of the speechless friend rolled over it, as in solemn ecstasy. Sometimes he said "Good! " when a bottle came in full; and sometimes he said "Ah! " when a bottle went out empty—and there his contributions to the gaiety of the evening ended.

Silence is occasionally infectious. Oppressed by private anxieties of their own, Marguerite and Vendale appeared to feel the influence of the speechless friend. The whole responsibility of keeping the talk going rested on Obenreizer's shoulders, and manfully did Obenreizer sustain it. He opened his heart in the character of an enlightened foreigner, and sang the praises of England. When other topics ran dry, he returned to this inexhaustible source, and always set the stream running again as copiously as ever. Obenreizer would have given an arm, an eye, or a leg to have been born an Englishman. Out of England there was no such institution as a home, no such thing as a fireside, no such object as a beautiful woman. His dear Miss Marguerite would excuse him, if he accounted for *her* attractions on the theory that English blood must have mixed at some former time with their obscure and unknown ancestry. Survey this English nation, and behold a tall, clean, plump, and solid people! Look at their cities! What magnificence in their public buildings! What admirable order and propriety in their streets! Admire their laws, combining the eternal principle of justice with the other eternal principle of pounds, shillings, and pence; and applying the product to all civil injuries, from an injury to a man's honour, to an injury to a man's nose! You have ruined my daughter—pounds, shillings, and pence! You have knocked me down with a blow in my face—pounds, shillings, and pence! Where was the material prosperity of such a country as *that* to stop? Obenreizer, projecting himself into the future, failed to see the end of it. Obenreizer's enthusiasm entreated permission to exhale itself, English fashion, in a toast. Here is our modest little dinner over, here is our frugal dessert on the table, and here is the admirer of England conforming to national customs, and making a speech! A toast to your white cliffs of Albion, Mr. Vendale! to your national virtues, your charming climate, and your fascinating women! to your Hearths, to your Homes, to your Habeas Corpus, and to all your other institutions! In one word—to England! Heep-heep-heep! hooray!

Obenreizer's voice had barely chanted the last note of the English cheer, the speechless friend had barely drained the last drop out of his glass, when the festive proceedings were interrupted by a modest tap at the door. A woman-servant came in, and approached her master with a little note in her hand. Obenreizer opened the note with a frown; and, after reading it with an expression of genuine annoyance, passed it on to his compatriot and friend. Vendale's spirits rose as he watched these proceedings. Had he found an ally in the annoying little note? Was the long-looked-for chance actually coming at last?

"I am afraid there is no help for it? " said Obenreizer, addressing his fellow-countryman. "I am afraid we must go. "

The speechless friend handed back the letter, shrugged his heavy shoulders, and poured himself out a last glass of wine. His fat fingers lingered fondly round the neck of the bottle. They pressed it with a little amatory squeeze at parting. His globular eyes looked dimly, as through an intervening haze, at Vendale and Marguerite. His heavy articulation laboured, and brought forth a whole sentence at a birth. "I think, " he said, "I should have liked a little more wine. " His breath failed him after that effort; he gasped, and walked to the door.

Obenreizer addressed himself to Vendale with an appearance of the deepest distress.

"I am so shocked, so confused, so distressed, " he began. "A misfortune has happened to one of my compatriots. He is alone, he is ignorant of your language—I and my good friend, here, have no choice but to go and help him. What can I say in my excuse? How can I describe my affliction at depriving myself in this way of the honour of your company? "

He paused, evidently expecting to see Vendale take up his hat and retire. Discerning his opportunity at last, Vendale determined to do nothing of the kind. He met Obenreizer dexterously, with Obenreizer's own weapons.

"Pray don't distress yourself, " he said. "I'll wait here with the greatest pleasure till you come back. "

Marguerite blushed deeply, and turned away to her embroidery-frame in a corner by the window. The film showed itself in Obenreizer's eyes, and the smile came something sourly to Obenreizer's lips. To have told Vendale that there was no reasonable prospect of his coming back in good time, would have been to risk offending a man whose favourable opinion was of solid commercial importance to him. Accepting his defeat with the best possible grace, he declared himself to be equally honoured and delighted by Vendale's proposal. "So frank, so friendly, so English! " He bustled about, apparently looking for something he wanted, disappeared for a moment through the folding-doors communicating with the next room, came back with his hat and coat, and protesting that he would return at the earliest possible moment, embraced Vendale's elbows, and vanished from the scene in company with the speechless friend.

Vendale turned to the corner by the window, in which Marguerite had placed herself with her work. There, as if she had dropped from the ceiling, or come up through the floor—there, in the old attitude, with her face to the stove—sat an Obstacle that had not been foreseen, in the person of Madame Dor! She half got up, half looked over her broad shoulder at Vendale, and plumped down again. Was she at work? Yes. Cleaning Obenreizer's gloves, as before? No; darning Obenreizer's stockings.

The case was now desperate. Two serious considerations presented themselves to Vendale. Was it possible to put Madame Dor into the stove? The stove wouldn't hold her. Was it possible to treat Madame Dor, not as a living woman, but as an article of furniture? Could the mind be brought to contemplate this respectable matron purely in the light of a chest of drawers, with a black gauze held-dress accidentally left on the top of it? Yes, the mind could be brought to do that. With a comparatively trifling effort, Vendale's mind did it. As he took his place on the old-fashioned window-seat, close by Marguerite and her embroidery, a slight movement appeared in the chest of drawers, but no remark issued from it. Let it be remembered that solid furniture is not easy to move, and that it has this advantage in consequence—there is no fear of upsetting it.

Unusually silent and unusually constrained—with the bright colour fast fading from her face, with a feverish energy possessing her fingers—the pretty Marguerite bent over her embroidery, and worked as if her life depended on it. Hardly less agitated himself, Vendale felt the importance of leading her very gently to the avowal which he was eager to make—to the other sweeter avowal still, which he was longing to hear. A woman's love is never to be taken by storm; it yields insensibly to a system of gradual approach. It ventures by the roundabout way, and listens to the low voice. Vendale led her memory back to their past meetings when they were travelling together in Switzerland. They revived the impressions, they recalled the events, of the happy bygone time. Little by little, Marguerite's constraint vanished. She smiled, she was interested, she looked at Vendale, she grew idle with her needle, she made false stitches in her work. Their voices sank lower and lower; their faces bent nearer and nearer to each other as they spoke. And Madame Dor? Madame Dor behaved like an angel. She never looked round; she never said a word; she went on with Obenreizer's stockings. Pulling each stocking up tight over her left arm, and holding that arm aloft from time to time, to catch the light on her work, there were moments—delicate and indescribable moments—when Madame Dor appeared to be sitting upside down, and contemplating one of her own respectable legs, elevated in the air. As the minutes wore on, these elevations followed each other at longer and longer intervals. Now and again, the black gauze head-dress nodded, dropped forward, recovered itself. A little heap of stockings slid softly from Madame Dor's lap, and remained unnoticed on the floor. A prodigious ball of worsted followed the stockings, and rolled lazily under the table. The black gauze head-dress nodded, dropped forward, recovered itself, nodded again, dropped forward again, and recovered itself no more. A composite sound, partly as of the purring of an immense cat, partly as of the planing of a soft board, rose over the hushed voices of the lovers, and hummed at regular intervals through the room. Nature and

Madame Dor had combined together in Vendale's interests. The best of women was asleep.

Marguerite rose to stop—not the snoring—let us say, the audible repose of Madame Dor. Vendale laid his hand on her arm, and pressed her back gently into her chair.

"Don't disturb her, " he whispered. "I have been waiting to tell you a secret. Let me tell it now. "

Marguerite resumed her seat. She tried to resume her needle. It was useless; her eyes failed her; her hand failed her; she could find nothing.

"We have been talking, " said Vendale, "of the happy time when we first met, and first travelled together. I have a confession to make. I have been concealing something. When we spoke of my first visit to Switzerland, I told you of all the impressions I had brought back with me to England—except one. Can you guess what that one is? "

Her eyes looked stedfastly at the embroidery, and her face turned a little away from him. Signs of disturbance began to appear in her neat velvet bodice, round the region of the brooch. She made no reply. Vendale pressed the question without mercy.

"Can you guess what the one Swiss impression is which I have not told you yet? "

Her face turned back towards him, and a faint smile trembled on her lips.

"An impression of the mountains, perhaps? " she said slyly.

"No; a much more precious impression than that. "

"Of the lakes? "

"No. The lakes have not grown dearer and dearer in remembrance to me every day. The lakes are not associated with my happiness in the present, and my hopes in the future. Marguerite! all that makes life worth having hangs, for me, on a word from your lips. Marguerite! I love you! "

Her head drooped as he took her hand. He drew her to him, and looked at her. The tears escaped from her downcast eyes, and fell slowly over her cheeks.

"O, Mr. Vendale, " she said sadly, "it would have been kinder to have kept your secret. Have you forgotten the distance between us? It can never, never be! "

"There can be but one distance between us, Marguerite—a distance of your making. My love, my darling, there is no higher rank in goodness, there is no higher rank in beauty, than yours! Come! whisper the one little word which tells me you will be my wife! "

She sighed bitterly. "Think of your family, " she murmured; "and think of mine! "

Vendale drew her a little nearer to him.

"If you dwell on such an obstacle as that, " he said, "I shall think but one thought—I shall think I have offended you. "

She started, and looked up. "O, no! " she exclaimed innocently. The instant the words passed her lips, she saw the construction that might be placed on them. Her confession had escaped her in spite of herself. A lovely flush of colour overspread her face. She made a momentary effort to disengage herself from her lover's embrace. She looked up at him entreatingly. She tried to speak. The words died on her lips in the kiss that Vendale pressed on them. "Let me go, Mr. Vendale! " she said faintly.

"Call me George. "

She laid her head on his bosom. All her heart went out to him at last. "George! " she whispered.

"Say you love me! "

Her arms twined themselves gently round his neck. Her lips, timidly touching his cheek, murmured the delicious words—"I love you! "

In the moment of silence that followed, the sound of the opening and closing of the house-door came clear to them through the wintry stillness of the street.

Marguerite started to her feet.

"Let me go! " she said. "He has come back! "

She hurried from the room, and touched Madame Dor's shoulder in passing. Madame Dor woke up with a loud snort, looked first over one shoulder and then over the other, peered down into her lap, and discovered neither stockings, worsted, nor darning-needle in it. At the same moment, footsteps became audible ascending the stairs. "Mon Dieu! " said Madame Dor, addressing herself to the stove, and trembling violently. Vendale picked up the stockings and the ball, and huddled them all back in a heap over her shoulder. "Mon Dieu! " said Madame Dor, for the second time, as the avalanche of worsted poured into her capacious lap.

The door opened, and Obenreizer came in. His first glance round the room showed him that Marguerite was absent.

"What! " he exclaimed, "my niece is away? My niece is not here to entertain you in my absence? This is unpardonable. I shall bring her back instantly. "

Vendale stopped him.

"I beg you will not disturb Miss Obenreizer, " he said. "You have returned, I see, without your friend? "

"My friend remains, and consoles our afflicted compatriot. A heart-rending scene, Mr. Vendale! The household gods at the pawnbroker's—the family immersed in tears. We all embraced in silence. My admirable friend alone possessed his composure. He sent out, on the spot, for a bottle of wine. "

"Can I say a word to you in private, Mr. Obenreizer? "

"Assuredly. " He turned to Madame Dor. "My good creature, you are sinking for want of repose. Mr. Vendale will excuse you. "

Madame Dor rose, and set forth sideways on her journey from the stove to bed. She dropped a stocking. Vendale picked it up for her, and opened one of the folding-doors. She advanced a step, and dropped three more stockings. Vendale stooping to recover them as before, Obenreizer interfered with profuse apologies, and with a warning look at Madame Dor. Madame Dor acknowledged the look by dropping the whole of the stockings in a heap, and then shuffling away panic-stricken from the scene of disaster. Obenreizer swept up the complete collection fiercely in both hands. "Go! " he cried, giving his prodigious handful a preparatory swing in the air. Madame Dor said, "Mon Dieu, " and vanished into the next room, pursued by a shower of stockings.

"What must you think, Mr. Vendale, " said Obenreizer, closing the door, "of this deplorable intrusion of domestic details? For myself, I blush at it. We are beginning the New Year as badly as possible; everything has gone wrong to-night. Be seated, pray—and say, what may I offer you? Shall we pay our best respects to another of your noble English institutions? It is my study to be, what you call, jolly. I propose a grog. "

Vendale declined the grog with all needful respect for that noble institution.

"I wish to speak to you on a subject in which I am deeply interested, " he said. "You must have observed, Mr. Obenreizer, that I have, from the first, felt no ordinary admiration for your charming niece? "

"You are very good. In my niece's name, I thank you. "

"Perhaps you may have noticed, latterly, that my admiration for Miss Obenreizer has grown into a tenderer and deeper feeling—? "

"Shall we say friendship, Mr. Vendale? "

"Say love—and we shall be nearer to the truth. "

Obenreizer started out of his chair. The faintly discernible beat, which was his nearest approach to a change of colour, showed itself suddenly in his cheeks.

"You are Miss Obenreizer's guardian, " pursued Vendale. "I ask you to confer upon me the greatest of all favours—I ask you to give me her hand in marriage. "

Obenreizer dropped back into his chair. "Mr. Vendale, " he said, "you petrify me. "

"I will wait, " rejoined Vendale, "until you have recovered yourself. "

"One word before I recover myself. You have said nothing about this to my niece? "

"I have opened my whole heart to your niece. And I have reason to hope—"

"What! " interposed Obenreizer. "You have made a proposal to my niece, without first asking for my authority to pay your addresses to her? " He struck his hand on the table, and lost his hold over himself for the first time in Vendale's experience of him. "Sir! " he exclaimed, indignantly, "what sort of conduct is this? As a man of honour, speaking to a man of honour, how can you justify it? "

"I can only justify it as one of our English institutions, " said Vendale quietly. "You admire our English institutions. I can't honestly tell you, Mr. Obenreizer, that I regret what I have done. I can only assure you that I have not acted in the matter with any intentional disrespect towards yourself. This said, may I ask you to tell me plainly what objection you see to favouring my suit? "

"I see this immense objection, " answered Obenreizer, "that my niece and you are not on a social equality together. My niece is the daughter of a poor peasant; and you are the son of a gentleman. You do us an honour, " he added, lowering himself again gradually to his customary polite level, "which deserves, and has, our most grateful acknowledgments. But the inequality is too glaring; the sacrifice is too great. You English are a proud people, Mr. Vendale. I have observed enough of this country to see that such a marriage as you propose would be a scandal here. Not a hand would be held out to your peasant-wife; and all your best friends would desert you. "

"One moment, " said Vendale, interposing on his side. "I may claim, without any great arrogance, to know more of my country people in general, and of my own friends in particular, than you do. In the estimation of everybody whose opinion is worth having, my wife herself would be the one sufficient justification of my marriage. If I did not feel certain—observe, I say certain—that I am offering her a position which she can accept without so much as the shadow of a humiliation—I would never (cost me what it might) have asked her to be my wife. Is there any other obstacle that you see? Have you any personal objection to me? "

Obenreizer spread out both his hands in courteous protest. "Personal objection! " he exclaimed. "Dear sir, the bare question is painful to me. "

"We are both men of business, " pursued Vendale, "and you naturally expect me to satisfy you that I have the means of supporting a wife. I can explain my pecuniary position in two words. I inherit from my parents a fortune of twenty thousand pounds. In half of that sum I have only a life-interest, to which, if I die, leaving a widow, my widow succeeds. If I die, leaving children, the money itself is divided among them, as they come of age. The other half of my fortune is at my own disposal, and is invested in the wine-business. I see my way to greatly improving that business. As it stands at present, I cannot state my return from my capital embarked at more than twelve hundred a year. Add the yearly value of my life-interest—and the total reaches a present annual income of fifteen hundred pounds. I have the fairest prospect of soon making it more. In the meantime, do you object to me on pecuniary grounds? "

Driven back to his last entrenchment, Obenreizer rose, and took a turn backwards and forwards in the room. For the moment, he was plainly at a loss what to say or do next.

"Before I answer that last question, " he said, after a little close consideration with himself, "I beg leave to revert for a moment to Miss Marguerite. You said something just now which seemed to imply that she returns the sentiment with which you are pleased to regard her? "

"I have the inestimable happiness, " said Vendale, "of knowing that she loves me. "

Obenreizer stood silent for a moment, with the film over his eyes, and the faintly perceptible beat becoming visible again in his cheeks.

"If you will excuse me for a few minutes, " he said, with ceremonious politeness, "I should like to have the opportunity of speaking to my niece. " With those words, he bowed, and quitted the room.

Left by himself, Vendale's thoughts (as a necessary result of the interview, thus far) turned instinctively to the consideration of Obenreizer's motives. He had put obstacles in the way of the courtship; he was now putting obstacles in the way of the marriage—a marriage offering advantages which even his ingenuity could not dispute. On the face of it, his conduct was incomprehensible. What did it mean?

Seeking, under the surface, for the answer to that question—and remembering that Obenreizer was a man of about his own age; also, that Marguerite was, strictly speaking, his half-niece only—Vendale asked himself, with a lover's ready jealousy, whether he had a rival to fear, as well as a guardian to conciliate. The thought just crossed his mind, and no more. The sense of Marguerite's kiss still lingering on his cheek reminded him gently that even the jealousy of a moment was now a treason to *her*.

On reflection, it seemed most likely that a personal motive of another kind might suggest the true explanation of Obenreizer's conduct. Marguerite's grace and beauty were precious ornaments in that little household. They gave it a special social attraction and a special social importance. They armed Obenreizer with a certain influence in reserve, which he could always depend upon to make his house attractive, and which he might always bring more or less to bear on the forwarding of his own private ends. Was he the sort of man to resign such advantages as were here implied, without obtaining the fullest possible compensation for the loss? A connection by marriage with Vendale offered him solid advantages, beyond all doubt. But there were hundreds of men in London with far greater power and far wider influence than Vendale possessed. Was it possible that this man's ambition secretly looked higher than the highest prospects that could be offered to him by the alliance now proposed for his niece? As the question passed through Vendale's mind, the man himself reappeared—to answer it, or not to answer it, as the event might prove.

A marked change was visible in Obenreizer when he resumed his place. His manner was less assured, and there were plain traces about his mouth of recent agitation which had not been successfully composed. Had he said something, referring either to Vendale or to himself, which had raised Marguerite's spirit, and which had placed him, for the first time, face to face with a resolute assertion of his niece's will? It might or might not be. This only was certain—he looked like a man who had met with a repulse.

"I have spoken to my niece, " he began. "I find, Mr. Vendale, that even your influence has not entirely blinded her to the social objections to your proposal. "

"May I ask, " returned Vendale, "if that is the only result of your interview with Miss Obenreizer? "

A momentary flash leapt out through the Obenreizer film.

"You are master of the situation, " he answered, in a tone of sardonic submission. "If you insist on my admitting it, I do admit it in those words. My niece's will and mine used to be one, Mr. Vendale. You have come between us, and her will is now yours. In my country, we know when we are beaten, and we submit with our best grace. I submit, with my best grace, on certain conditions. Let us revert to the statement of your pecuniary position. I have an objection to you, my dear sir—a most amazing, a most audacious objection, from a man in my position to a man in yours. "

"What is it? "

"You have honoured me by making a proposal for my niece's hand. For the present (with best thanks and respects), I beg to decline it. "

"Why? "

"Because you are not rich enough. "

The objection, as the speaker had foreseen, took Vendale completely by surprise. For the moment he was speechless.

"Your income is fifteen hundred a year, " pursued Obenreizer. "In my miserable country I should fall on my knees before your income, and say, 'What a princely fortune! ' In wealthy England, I sit as I am, and say, 'A modest independence, dear sir; nothing more. Enough, perhaps, for a wife in your own rank of life who has no social prejudices to conquer. Not more than half enough for a wife who is a meanly born foreigner, and who has all your social prejudices against her. ' Sir! if my niece is ever to marry you, she will have what you call uphill work of it in taking her place at starting. Yes, yes; this is not your view, but it remains, immovably remains, my view for all that. For my niece's sake, I claim that this uphill work shall be made as smooth as possible. Whatever material advantages she can have to help her, ought, in common justice, to be hers. Now, tell me, Mr. Vendale, on your fifteen hundred a year can your wife have a house in a fashionable quarter, a footman to open her door, a butler to wait at her table, and a carriage and horses to drive about in? I see the answer in your face—your face says, No. Very good. Tell me one more thing, and I have done. Take the mass of your educated, accomplished, and lovely country-women, is it, or is it not, the fact that a lady who has a house in a fashionable quarter, a footman to open her door, a butler to wait at her table, and a carriage and horses to drive about in, is a lady who has gained four steps, in female estimation, at starting? Yes? or No? "

"Come to the point, " said Vendale. "You view this question as a question of terms. What are your terms? "

"The lowest terms, dear sir, on which you can provide your wife with those four steps at starting. Double your present income—the most rigid economy cannot do it in England on less. You said just now that you expected greatly to increase the value of your business. To work—and increase it! I am a good devil after all! On the day when you satisfy me, by plain proofs, that your income has risen to three thousand a year, ask me for my niece's hand, and it is yours. "

"May I inquire if you have mentioned this arrangement to Miss Obenreizer? "

"Certainly. She has a last little morsel of regard still left for me, Mr. Vendale, which is not yours yet; and she accepts my terms. In other words, she submits to be guided by her guardian's regard for her welfare, and by her guardian's superior knowledge of the world. " He threw himself back in his chair, in firm reliance on his position, and in full possession of his excellent temper.

Any open assertion of his own interests, in the situation in which Vendale was now placed, seemed to be (for the present at least) hopeless. He found himself literally left with no ground to stand on. Whether Obenreizer's objections were the genuine product of Obenreizer's own view of the case, or whether he was simply delaying the marriage in the hope of ultimately breaking it off altogether—in either of these events, any present resistance on Vendale's part would be equally useless. There was no help for it but to yield, making the best terms that he could on his own side.

"I protest against the conditions you impose on me, " he began.

"Naturally, " said Obenreizer; "I dare say I should protest, myself, in your place. "

"Say, however, " pursued Vendale, "that I accept your terms. In that case, I must be permitted to make two stipulations on my part. In the first place, I shall expect to be allowed to see your niece. "

"Aha! to see my niece? and to make her in as great a hurry to be married as you are yourself? Suppose I say, No? you would see her perhaps without my permission? "

"Decidedly! "

"How delightfully frank! How exquisitely English! You shall see her, Mr. Vendale, on certain days, which we will appoint together. What next? "

"Your objection to my income, " proceeded Vendale, "has taken me completely by surprise. I wish to be assured against any repetition of that surprise. Your present views of my qualification for marriage require me to have an income of three thousand a year. Can I be certain, in the future, as your experience of England enlarges, that your estimate will rise no higher? "

"In plain English, " said Obenreizer, "you doubt my word? "

"Do you purpose to take *my* word for it when I inform you that I have doubled my income? " asked Vendale. "If my memory does not deceive me, you stipulated, a minute since, for plain proofs? "

"Well played, Mr. Vendale! You combine the foreign quickness with the English solidity. Accept my best congratulations. Accept, also, my written guarantee. "

He rose; seated himself at a writing-desk at a side-table, wrote a few lines, and presented them to Vendale with a low bow. The engagement was perfectly explicit, and was signed and dated with scrupulous care.

"Are you satisfied with your guarantee? "

"I am satisfied. "

"Charmed to hear it, I am sure. We have had our little skirmish—we have really been wonderfully clever on both sides. For the present our affairs are settled. I bear no malice. You bear no malice. Come, Mr. Vendale, a good English shake hands. "

Vendale gave his hand, a little bewildered by Obenreizer's sudden transitions from one humour to another.

"When may I expect to see Miss Obenreizer again? " he asked, as he rose to go.

"Honour me with a visit to-morrow, " said Obenreizer, "and we will settle it then. Do have a grog before you go! No? Well! well! we will reserve the grog till you have your three thousand a year, and are ready to be married. Aha! When will that be? "

"I made an estimate, some months since, of the capacities of my business, " said Vendale. "If that estimate is correct, I shall double my present income—"

"And be married! " added Obenreizer.

"And be married, " repeated Vendale, "within a year from this time. Good- night. "

## VENDALE MAKES MISCHIEF

When Vendale entered his office the next morning, the dull commercial routine at Cripple Corner met him with a new face. Marguerite had an interest in it now! The whole machinery which Wilding's death had set in motion, to realise the value of the business—the balancing of ledgers, the estimating of debts, the taking of stock, and the rest of it—was now transformed into machinery which indicated the chances for and against a speedy marriage. After looking over results, as presented by his accountant, and checking additions and subtractions, as rendered by the clerks, Vendale turned his attention to the stock-taking department next, and sent a message to the cellars, desiring to see the report.

The Cellarman's appearance, the moment he put his head in at the door of his master's private room, suggested that something very extraordinary must have happened that morning. There was an approach to alacrity in Joey Ladle's movements! There was something which actually simulated cheerfulness in Joey Ladle's face

"What's the matter? " asked Vendale. "Anything wrong? "

"I should wish to mention one thing, " answered Joey. "Young Mr. Vendale, I have never set myself up for a prophet. "

"Who ever said you did? "

"No prophet, as far as I've heard I tell of that profession, " proceeded Joey, "ever lived principally underground. No prophet, whatever else he might take in at the pores, ever took in wine from morning to night, for a number of years together. When I said to young Master Wilding, respecting his changing the name of the firm, that one of these days he might find he'd changed the luck of the firm—did I put myself forward as a prophet? No, I didn't. Has what I said to him come true? Yes, it has. In the time of Pebbleson Nephew, Young Mr. Vendale, no such thing was ever known as a mistake made in a consignment delivered at these doors. There's a mistake been made now. Please to remark that it happened before Miss Margaret came here. For which reason it don't go against what I've said respecting Miss Margaret singing round the luck. Read that, sir, " concluded Joey, pointing attention to a special passage in the report, with a forefinger which appeared to be in process of taking in through the pores nothing more remarkable than dirt. "It's foreign to my nature to crow over the house I serve, but I feel it a kind of solemn duty to ask you to read that. "

Vendale read as follows: —"Note, respecting the Swiss champagne. An irregularity has been discovered in the last consignment received from the firm of Defresnier and Co. " Vendale stopped, and referred to a memorandum-book by his side. "That was in Mr. Wilding's time, " he said. "The vintage was a particularly good one, and he took the whole of it. The Swiss champagne has done very well, hasn't it? "

"I don't say it's done badly, " answered the Cellarman. "It may have got sick in our customers' bins, or it may have bust in our customers' hands. But I don't say it's done badly with us. "

Vendale resumed the reading of the note: "We find the number of the cases to be quite correct by the books. But six of them, which present a slight difference from the rest in the brand, have been opened, and have been found to contain a red wine instead of champagne. The similarity in the brands, we suppose, caused a mistake to be made in sending the consignment from Neuchatel. The error has not been found to extend beyond six cases. "

"Is that all! " exclaimed Vendale, tossing the note away from him.

Joey Ladle's eye followed the flying morsel of paper drearily.

"I'm glad to see you take it easy, sir, " he said. "Whatever happens, it will be always a comfort to you to remember that you took it easy at first. Sometimes one mistake leads to another. A man drops a bit of orange-peel on the pavement by mistake, and another man treads on it by mistake, and there's a job at the hospital, and a party crippled for life. I'm glad you take it easy, sir. In Pebbleson Nephew's time we shouldn't have taken it easy till we had seen the end of it. Without desiring to crow over the house, young Mr. Vendale, I wish you well through it. No offence, sir, " said the Cellarman, opening the door to go out, and looking in again ominously before he shut it. "I'm muddled and molloncolly, I grant you. But I'm an old servant of Pebbleson Nephew, and I wish you well through them six cases of red wine. "

Left by himself, Vendale laughed, and took up his pen. "I may as well send a line to Defresnier and Company, " he thought, "before I forget it. " He wrote at once in these terms:

"Dear Sirs. We are taking stock, and a trifling mistake has been discovered in the last consignment of champagne sent by your house to ours. Six of the cases contain red wine — which we hereby return to you. The matter can easily be set right, either by your sending us six cases of the champagne, if they can be produced, or, if not, by your crediting us with the value of six cases on the amount last paid (five hundred pounds) by our firm to yours. Your faithful servants,

"WILDING AND CO. "

This letter despatched to the post, the subject dropped at once out of Vendale's mind. He had other and far more interesting matters to think of. Later in the day he paid the visit to Obenreizer which had been agreed on between them. Certain evenings in the week were set apart which he was privileged to spend with Marguerite—always, however, in the presence of a third person. On this stipulation Obenreizer politely but positively insisted. The one concession he made was to give Vendale his choice of who the third person should be. Confiding in past experience, his choice fell unhesitatingly upon the excellent woman who mended Obenreizer's stockings. On hearing of the responsibility entrusted to her, Madame Dor's intellectual nature burst suddenly into a new stage of development. She waited till Obenreizer's eye was off her—and then she looked at Vendale, and dimly winked.

The time passed—the happy evenings with Marguerite came and went. It was the tenth morning since Vendale had written to the Swiss firm, when the answer appeared, on his desk, with the other letters of the day:

"Dear Sirs. We beg to offer our excuses for the little mistake which has happened. At the same time, we regret to add that the statement of our error, with which you have favoured us, has led to a very unexpected discovery. The affair is a most serious one for you and for us. The particulars are as follows:

"Having no more champagne of the vintage last sent to you, we made arrangements to credit your firm to the value of six cases, as suggested by yourself. On taking this step, certain forms observed in our mode of doing business necessitated a reference to our bankers' book, as well as to our ledger. The result is a moral certainty that no such remittance as you mention can have reached our house, and a literal certainty that no such remittance has been paid to our account at the bank.

"It is needless, at this stage of the proceedings, to trouble you with details. The money has unquestionably been stolen in the course of its transit from you to us. Certain peculiarities which we observe, relating to the manner in which the fraud has been perpetrated, lead us to conclude that the thief may have calculated on being able to pay the missing sum to our bankers, before an inevitable discovery followed the annual striking of our balance. This would not have happened, in the usual course, for another three months. During that period, but for your letter, we might have remained perfectly unconscious of the robbery that has been committed.

"We mention this last circumstance, as it may help to show you that we have to do, in this case, with no ordinary thief. Thus far we have not even a suspicion of who that thief is. But we believe you will assist us in making some advance towards discovery, by examining the receipt (forged, of course) which has no doubt purported to come to you from our house. Be pleased to look and see whether it is a receipt entirely in manuscript, or whether it is a numbered and printed form which merely requires the filling in of the amount. The settlement of this apparently trivial question is, we assure you, a matter of vital importance. Anxiously awaiting your reply, we remain, with high esteem and consideration,

"DEFRESNIER & CIE. "

Vendale had the letter on his desk, and waited a moment to steady his mind under the shock that had fallen on it. At the time of all others when it was most important to him to increase the value of his business, that business was threatened with a loss of five hundred pounds. He thought of Marguerite, as he took the key from his pocket and opened the iron chamber in the wall in which the books and papers of the firm were kept.

He was still in the chamber, searching for the forged receipt, when he was startled by a voice speaking close behind him.

"A thousand pardons, " said the voice; "I am afraid I disturb you. "

He turned, and found himself face to face with Marguerite's guardian.

"I have called, " pursued Obenreizer, "to know if I can be of any use. Business of my own takes me away for some days to Manchester and Liverpool. Can I combine any business of yours with it? I am entirely at your disposal, in the character of commercial traveller for the firm of Wilding and Co. "

"Excuse me for one moment, " said Vendale; "I will speak to you directly. " He turned round again, and continued his search among the papers. "You come at a time when friendly offers are more than usually precious to me, " he resumed. "I have had very bad news this morning from Neuchatel. "

"Bad news, " exclaimed Obenreizer. "From Defresnier and Company? "

"Yes. A remittance we sent to them has been stolen. I am threatened with a loss of five hundred pounds. What's that? "

Turning sharply, and looking into the room for the second time, Vendale discovered his envelope case overthrown on the floor, and Obenreizer on his knees picking up the contents.

"All my awkwardness, " said Obenreizer. "This dreadful news of yours startled me; I stepped back—" He became too deeply interested in collecting the scattered envelopes to finish the sentence.

"Don't trouble yourself, " said Vendale. "The clerk will pick the things up. "

"This dreadful news! " repeated Obenreizer, persisting in collecting the envelopes. "This dreadful news! "

"If you will read the letter, " said Vendale, "you will find I have exaggerated nothing. There it is, open on my desk. "

He resumed his search, and in a moment more discovered the forged receipt. It was on the numbered and printed form, described by the Swiss firm. Vendale made a memorandum of the number and the date. Having replaced the receipt and locked up the iron chamber, he had leisure to notice Obenreizer, reading the letter in the recess of a window at the far end of the room.

"Come to the fire, " said Vendale. "You look perished with the cold out there. I will ring for some more coals. "

Obenreizer rose, and came slowly back to the desk. "Marguerite will be as sorry to hear of this as I am, " he said, kindly. "What do you mean to do? "

"I am in the hands of Defresnier and Company, " answered Vendale. "In my total ignorance of the circumstances, I can only do what they recommend. The receipt which I have just found, turns out to be the numbered and printed form. They seem to attach some special importance to its discovery. You have had experience, when you were in the Swiss house, of their way of doing business. Can you guess what object they have in view? "

Obenreizer offered a suggestion.

"Suppose I examine the receipt? " he said.

"Are you ill? " asked Vendale, startled by the change in his face, which now showed itself plainly for the first time. "Pray go to the fire. You seem to be shivering—I hope you are not going to be ill? "

"Not I! " said Obenreizer. "Perhaps I have caught cold. Your English climate might have spared an admirer of your English institutions. Let me look at the receipt. "

Vendale opened the iron chamber. Obenreizer took a chair, and drew it close to the fire. He held both hands over the flames. "Let me look at the receipt, " he repeated, eagerly, as Vendale reappeared with the paper in his hand. At the same moment a porter entered the room with a fresh supply of coals. Vendale told him to make a good fire. The man obeyed the order with a disastrous alacrity. As he stepped forward and raised the scuttle, his foot caught in a fold of the rug, and he discharged his entire cargo of coals into the grate. The result was an instant smothering of the flame, and the production of a stream of yellow smoke, without a visible morsel of fire to account for it.

"Imbecile! " whispered Obenreizer to himself, with a look at the man which the man remembered for many a long day afterwards.

"Will you come into the clerks' room? " asked Vendale. "They have a stove there. "

"No, no. No matter. "

Vendale handed him the receipt. Obenreizer's interest in examining it appeared to have been quenched as suddenly and as effectually as the fire itself. He just glanced over the document, and said, "No; I don't understand it! I am sorry to be of no use. "

"I will write to Neuchatel by to-night's post, " said Vendale, putting away the receipt for the second time. "We must wait, and see what comes of it. "

"By to-night's post, " repeated Obenreizer. "Let me see. You will get the answer in eight or nine days' time. I shall be back before that. If I can be of any service, as commercial traveller, perhaps you will let me know between this and then. You will send me written instructions? My best thanks. I shall be most anxious for your answer from Neuchatel. Who knows? It may be a mistake, my dear friend, after all. Courage! courage! courage! " He had entered the room with no appearance of being pressed for time. He now snatched up his hat, and took his leave with the air of a man who had not another moment to lose.

Left by himself, Vendale took a turn thoughtfully in the room.

His previous impression of Obenreizer was shaken by what he had heard and seen at the interview which had just taken place. He was disposed, for the first time, to doubt whether, in this case, he had not been a little hasty and hard in his judgment on another man. Obenreizer's surprise and regret, on hearing the news from Neuchatel, bore the plainest marks of being honestly felt—not politely assumed for the occasion. With troubles of his own to encounter, suffering, to all appearance, from the first insidious attack of a serious illness, he had looked and spoken like a man who really deplored the disaster that had fallen on his friend. Hitherto Vendale had tried vainly to alter his first opinion of Marguerite's guardian, for Marguerite's sake. All the generous instincts in his nature now combined together and shook the evidence which had seemed unanswerable up to this time. "Who knows? " he thought. "I may have read that man's face wrongly, after all. "

The time passed—the happy evenings with Marguerite came and went. It was again the tenth morning since Vendale had written to the Swiss firm; and again the answer appeared on his desk with the other letters of the day:

"Dear Sir. My senior partner, M. Defresnier, has been called away, by urgent business, to Milan. In his absence (and with his full concurrence and authority), I now write to you again on the subject of the missing five hundred pounds.

"Your discovery that the forged receipt is executed upon one of our numbered and printed forms has caused inexpressible surprise and distress to my partner and to myself. At the time when your remittance was stolen, but three keys were in existence opening the strong-box in which our receipt-forms are invariably kept. My partner had one key; I had the other. The third was in the possession of a gentleman who, at that period, occupied a position of trust in our house. We should as soon have thought of suspecting one of ourselves as of suspecting this person. Suspicion now points at him, nevertheless. I cannot prevail on myself to inform you who the person is, so long as there is the shadow of a chance that he may come innocently out of the inquiry which must now be instituted. Forgive my silence; the motive of it is good.

"The form our investigation must now take is simple enough. The handwriting of your receipt must be compared, by competent persons whom we have at our disposal, with certain specimens of handwriting in our possession. I cannot send you the specimens for business reasons, which, when you hear them, you are sure to approve. I must beg you to send me the receipt to Neuchatel—and, in making this request, I must accompany it by a word of necessary warning.

"If the person, at whom suspicion now points, really proves to be the person who has committed this forger and theft, I have reason to fear that circumstances may have already put him on his guard. The only evidence against him is the evidence in your hands, and he will move heaven and earth to obtain and destroy it. I strongly urge you not to trust the receipt to the post. Send it to me, without loss of time, by a private hand, and choose nobody for your messenger but a person long established in your own employment, accustomed to travelling, capable of speaking French; a man of courage, a man of honesty, and, above all things, a man who can be trusted to let no stranger scrape acquaintance with him on the route. Tell no one—absolutely no one—but your messenger of the turn this matter has now taken. The safe transit of the receipt may depend on your interpreting *literally* the advice which I give you at the end of this letter.

"I have only to add that every possible saving of time is now of the last importance. More than one of our receipt-forms is missing—and it is impossible to say what new frauds may not be committed if we fail to lay our hands on the thief.

Your faithful servant
ROLLAND,
(Signing for Defresnier and Cie. )

Who was the suspected man? In Vendale's position, it seemed useless to inquire.

Who was to be sent to Neuchatel with the receipt? Men of courage and men of honesty were to be had at Cripple Corner for the asking. But where was the man who was accustomed to foreign travelling, who could speak the French language, and who could be really relied on to let no stranger scrape acquaintance with him on his route? There was but one man at hand who combined all those requisites in his own person, and that man was Vendale himself.

It was a sacrifice to leave his business; it was a greater sacrifice to leave Marguerite. But a matter of five hundred pounds was involved in the pending inquiry; and a literal interpretation of M. Rolland's advice was insisted on in terms which there was no trifling with. The more Vendale thought of it, the more plainly the necessity faced him, and said, "Go! "

As he locked up the letter with the receipt, the association of ideas reminded him of Obenreizer. A guess at the identity of the suspected man looked more possible now. Obenreizer might know.

The thought had barely passed through his mind, when the door opened, and Obenreizer entered the room.

"They told me at Soho Square you were expected back last night, " said Vendale, greeting him. "Have you done well in the country? Are you better? "

A thousand thanks. Obenreizer had done admirably well; Obenreizer was infinitely better. And now, what news? Any letter from Neuchatel?

"A very strange letter, " answered Vendale. "The matter has taken a new turn, and the letter insists — without excepting anybody — on my keeping our next proceedings a profound secret. "

"Without excepting anybody? " repeated Obenreizer. As he said the words, he walked away again, thoughtfully, to the window at the other end of the room, looked out for a moment, and suddenly came back to Vendale. "Surely they must have forgotten? " he resumed, "or they would have excepted me? "

"It is Monsieur Rolland who writes, " said Vendale. "And, as you say, he must certainly have forgotten. That view of the matter quite escaped me. I was just wishing I had you to consult, when you came into the room. And here I am tried by a formal prohibition, which cannot possibly have been intended to include you. How very annoying! "

Obenreizer's filmy eyes fixed on Vendale attentively.

"Perhaps it is more than annoying! " he said. "I came this morning not only to hear the news, but to offer myself as messenger, negotiator — what you will. Would you believe it? I have letters which oblige me to go to Switzerland immediately. Messages, documents, anything — I could have taken them all to Defresnier and Rolland for you. "

"You are the very man I wanted, " returned Vendale. "I had decided, most unwillingly, on going to Neuchatel myself, not five minutes since, because I could find no one here capable of taking my place. Let me look at the letter again. "

He opened the strong room to get at the letter. Obenreizer, after first glancing round him to make sure that they were alone, followed a step or two and waited, measuring Vendale with his eye. Vendale was the tallest man, and unmistakably the strongest man also of the two. Obenreizer turned away, and warmed himself at the fire.

Meanwhile, Vendale read the last paragraph in the letter for the third time. There was the plain warning — there was the closing sentence, which insisted on a literal interpretation of it. The hand, which was leading Vendale in the dark, led him on that condition only. A large sum was at stake: a terrible suspicion remained to be verified. If he acted on his own responsibility, and if anything happened to defeat the object in view, who would be blamed? As a man of business, Vendale had but one course to follow. He locked the letter up again.

"It is most annoying, " he said to Obenreizer—"it is a piece of forgetfulness on Monsieur Rolland's part which puts me to serious inconvenience, and places me in an absurdly false position towards you. What am I to do? I am acting in a very serious matter, and acting entirely in the dark. I have no choice but to be guided, not by the spirit, but by the letter of my instructions. You understand me, I am sure? You know, if I had not been fettered in this way, how gladly I should have accepted your services? "

"Say no more! " returned Obenreizer. "In your place I should have done the same. My good friend, I take no offence. I thank you for your compliment. We shall be travelling companions, at any rate, " added Obenreizer. "You go, as I go, at once? "

"At once. I must speak to Marguerite first, of course! "

"Surely! surely! Speak to her this evening. Come, and pick me up on the way to the station. We go together by the mail train to-night? "

"By the mail train to-night. "

\* \* \* \* \*

It was later than Vendale had anticipated when he drove up to the house in Soho Square. Business difficulties, occasioned by his sudden departure, had presented themselves by dozens. A cruelly large share of the time which he had hoped to devote to Marguerite had been claimed by duties at his office which it was impossible to neglect.

To his surprise and delight, she was alone in the drawing-room when he entered it.

"We have only a few minutes, George, " she said. "But Madame Dor has been good to me—and we can have those few minutes alone. "

She threw her arms round his neck, and whispered eagerly, "Have you done anything to offend Mr. Obenreizer? "

"I! " exclaimed Vendale, in amazement.

"Hush! " she said, "I want to whisper it. You know the little photograph I have got of you. This afternoon it happened to be on the chimney-piece. He took it up and looked at it—and I saw his face in the glass. I know you have offended him! He is merciless; he is revengeful; he is as secret as the grave. Don't go with him, George— don't go with him! "

"My own love, " returned Vendale, "you are letting your fancy frighten you! Obenreizer and I were never better friends than we are at this moment. "

Before a word more could be said, the sudden movement of some ponderous body shook the floor of the next room. The shock was followed by the appearance of Madame Dor. "Obenreizer" exclaimed this excellent person in a whisper, and plumped down instantly in her regular place by the stove.

Obenreizer came in with a courier's big strapped over his shoulder. "Are you ready? " he asked, addressing Vendale. "Can I take anything for you? You have no travelling-bag. I have got one. Here is the compartment for papers, open at your service. "

"Thank you, " said Vendale. "I have only one paper of importance with me; and that paper I am bound to take charge of myself. Here it is, " he added, touching the breast-pocket of his coat, "and here it must remain till we get to Neuchatel. "

As he said those words, Marguerite's hand caught his, and pressed it significantly. She was looking towards Obenreizer. Before Vendale could look, in his turn, Obenreizer had wheeled round, and was taking leave of Madame Dor.

"Adieu, my charming niece! " he said, turning to Marguerite next. "En route, my friend, for Neuchatel! " He tapped Vendale lightly over the breast-pocket of his coat and led the way to the door.

Vendale's last look was for Marguerite. Marguerite's last words to him were, "Don't go! "

## ACT III.

## IN THE VALLEY

It was about the middle of the month of February when Vendale and Obenreizer set forth on their expedition. The winter being a hard one, the time was bad for travellers. So bad was it that these two travellers, coming to Strasbourg, found its great inns almost empty. And even the few people they did encounter in that city, who had started from England or from Paris on business journeys towards the interior of Switzerland, were turning back.

Many of the railroads in Switzerland that tourists pass easily enough now, were almost or quite impracticable then. Some were not begun; more were not completed. On such as were open, there were still large gaps of old road where communication in the winter season was often stopped; on others, there were weak points where the new work was not safe, either under conditions of severe frost, or of rapid thaw. The running of trains on this last class was not to be counted on in the worst time of the year, was contingent upon weather, or was wholly abandoned through the months considered the most dangerous.

At Strasbourg there were more travellers' stories afloat, respecting the difficulties of the way further on, than there were travellers to relate them. Many of these tales were as wild as usual; but the more modestly marvellous did derive some colour from the circumstance that people were indisputably turning back. However, as the road to Basle was open, Vendale's resolution to push on was in no wise disturbed. Obenreizer's resolution was necessarily Vendale's, seeing that he stood at bay thus desperately: He must be ruined, or must destroy the evidence that Vendale carried about him, even if he destroyed Vendale with it.

The state of mind of each of these two fellow-travellers towards the other was this. Obenreizer, encircled by impending ruin through Vendale's quickness of action, and seeing the circle narrowed every hour by Vendale's energy, hated him with the animosity of a fierce cunning lower animal. He had always had instinctive movements in his breast against him; perhaps, because of that old sore of gentleman and peasant; perhaps, because of the openness of his nature, perhaps, because of his better looks; perhaps, because of his success with Marguerite; perhaps, on all those grounds, the two last not the least. And now he saw in him, besides, the hunter who was tracking him down. Vendale, on the other hand, always contending generously against his first vague mistrust, now felt bound to contend against it more than ever: reminding himself, "He is Marguerite's guardian. We are on perfectly friendly terms; he is my companion of his own proposal, and can have no interested motive in sharing this undesirable journey. " To which pleas in behalf of Obenreizer, chance added one consideration more, when they came to Basle after a journey of more than twice the average duration.

They had had a late dinner, and were alone in an inn room there, overhanging the Rhine: at that place rapid and deep, swollen and loud. Vendale lounged upon a couch, and Obenreizer walked to and fro: now, stopping at the window, looking at the crooked reflection of the town lights in the dark water (and peradventure thinking, "If I could fling him into it! "); now, resuming his walk with his eyes upon the floor.

"Where shall I rob him, if I can? Where shall I murder him, if I must? " So, as he paced the room, ran the river, ran the river, ran the river.

The burden seemed to him, at last, to be growing so plain, that he stopped; thinking it as well to suggest another burden to his companion.

"The Rhine sounds to-night, " he said with a smile, "like the old waterfall at home. That waterfall which my mother showed to travellers (I told you of it once). The sound of it changed with the weather, as does the sound of all falling waters and flowing waters. When I was pupil of the watchmaker, I remembered it as sometimes saying to me for whole days, 'Who are you, my little wretch? Who are you, my little wretch? ' I remembered it as saying, other times, when its sound was hollow, and storm was coming up the Pass: 'Boom, boom, boom. Beat him, beat him, beat him. ' Like my mother enraged—if she was my mother. "

"If she was? " said Vendale, gradually changing his attitude to a sitting one. "If she was? Why do you say 'if'? "

"What do I know? " replied the other negligently, throwing up his hands and letting them fall as they would. "What would you have? I am so obscurely born, that how can I say? I was very young, and all

the rest of the family were men and women, and my so-called
parents were old. Anything is possible of a case like that. "

"Did you ever doubt—"

"I told you once, I doubt the marriage of those two, " he replied,
throwing up his hands again, as if he were throwing the unprofitable
subject away. "But here I am in Creation. *I* come of no fine family.
What does it matter? "

"At least you are Swiss, " said Vendale, after following him with his
eyes to and fro.

"How do I know? " he retorted abruptly, and stopping to look back
over his shoulder. "I say to you, at least you are English. How do
you know? "

"By what I have been told from infancy. "

"Ah! I know of myself that way. "

"And, " added Vendale, pursuing the thought that he could not
drive back, "by my earliest recollections. "

"I also. I know of myself that way—if that way satisfies. "

"Does it not satisfy you? "

"It must. There is nothing like 'it must' in this little world. It must.
Two short words those, but stronger than long proof or reasoning. "

"You and poor Wilding were born in the same year. You were nearly
of an age, " said Vendale, again thoughtfully looking after him as he
resumed his pacing up and down.

"Yes. Very nearly. "

Could Obenreizer be the missing man? In the unknown associations
of things, was there a subtler meaning than he himself thought, in
that theory so often on his lips about the smallness of the world?
Had the Swiss letter presenting him followed so close on Mrs.
Goldstraw's revelation concerning the infant who had been taken
away to Switzerland, because he was that infant grown a man? In a

world where so many depths lie unsounded, it might be. The chances, or the laws—call them either—that had wrought out the revival of Vendale's own acquaintance with Obenreizer, and had ripened it into intimacy, and had brought them here together this present winter night, were hardly less curious; while read by such a light, they were seen to cohere towards the furtherance of a continuous and an intelligible purpose.

Vendale's awakened thoughts ran high while his eyes musingly followed Obenreizer pacing up and down the room, the river ever running to the tune: "Where shall I rob him, if I can? Where shall I murder him, if I must? " The secret of his dead friend was in no hazard from Vendale's lips; but just as his friend had died of its weight, so did he in his lighter succession feel the burden of the trust, and the obligation to follow any clue, however obscure. He rapidly asked himself, would he like this man to be the real Wilding? No. Argue down his mistrust as he might, he was unwilling to put such a substitute in the place of his late guileless, outspoken childlike partner. He rapidly asked himself, would he like this man to be rich? No. He had more power than enough over Marguerite as it was, and wealth might invest him with more. Would he like this man to be Marguerite's Guardian, and yet proved to stand in no degree of relationship towards her, however disconnected and distant? No. But these were not considerations to come between him and fidelity to the dead. Let him see to it that they passed him with no other notice than the knowledge that they *had* passed him, and left him bent on the discharge of a solemn duty. And he did see to it, so soon that he followed his companion with ungrudging eyes, while he still paced the room; that companion, whom he supposed to be moodily reflecting on his own birth, and not on another man's—least of all what man's—violent Death.

The road in advance from Basle to Neuchatel was better than had been represented. The latest weather had done it good. Drivers, both of horses and mules, had come in that evening after dark, and had reported nothing more difficult to be overcome than trials of patience, harness, wheels, axles, and whipcord. A bargain was soon struck for a carriage and horses, to take them on in the morning, and to start before daylight.

"Do you lock your door at night when travelling? " asked Obenreizer, standing warming his hands by the wood fire in Vendale's chamber, before going to his own.

"Not I. I sleep too soundly. "

"You are so sound a sleeper? " he retorted, with an admiring look. "What a blessing! "

"Anything but a blessing to the rest of the house, " rejoined Vendale, "if I had to be knocked up in the morning from the outside of my bedroom door. "

"I, too, " said Obenreizer, "leave open my room. But let me advise you, as a Swiss who knows: always, when you travel in my country, put your papers—and, of course, your money—under your pillow. Always the same place. "

"You are not complimentary to your countrymen, " laughed Vendale.

"My countrymen, " said Obenreizer, with that light touch of his friend's elbows by way of Good-Night and benediction, "I suppose are like the majority of men. And the majority of men will take what they can get. Adieu! At four in the morning. "

"Adieu! At four. "

Left to himself, Vendale raked the logs together, sprinkled over them the white wood-ashes lying on the hearth, and sat down to compose his thoughts. But they still ran high on their latest theme, and the running of the river tended to agitate rather than to quiet them. As he sat thinking, what little disposition he had had to sleep departed. He felt it hopeless to lie down yet, and sat dressed by the fire. Marguerite, Wilding, Obenreizer, the business he was then upon, and a thousand hopes and doubts that had nothing to do with it, occupied his mind at once. Everything seemed to have power over him but slumber. The departed disposition to sleep kept far away.

He had sat for a long time thinking, on the hearth, when his candle burned down and its light went out. It was of little moment; there was light enough in the fire. He changed his attitude, and, leaning his arm on the chair-back, and his chin upon that hand, sat thinking still.

But he sat between the fire and the bed, and, as the fire flickered in the play of air from the fast-flowing river, his enlarged shadow fluttered on the white wall by the bedside. His attitude gave it an air, half of mourning and half of bending over the bed imploring. His eyes were observant of it, when he became troubled by the disagreeable fancy that it was like Wilding's shadow, and not his own.

A slight change of place would cause it to disappear. He made the change, and the apparition of his disturbed fancy vanished. He now sat in the shade of a little nook beside the fire, and the door of the room was before him.

It had a long cumbrous iron latch. He saw the latch slowly and softly rise. The door opened a very little, and came to again, as though only the air had moved it. But he saw that the latch was out of the hasp.

The door opened again very slowly, until it opened wide enough to admit some one. It afterwards remained still for a while, as though cautiously held open on the other side. The figure of a man then entered, with its face turned towards the bed, and stood quiet just within the door. Until it said, in a low half-whisper, at the same time taking one stop forward: "Vendale! "

"What now? " he answered, springing from his seat; "who is it? "

It was Obenreizer, and he uttered a cry of surprise as Vendale came upon him from that unexpected direction. "Not in bed? " he said, catching him by both shoulders with an instinctive tendency to a struggle. "Then something *is* wrong! "

"What do you mean? " said Vendale, releasing himself.

"First tell me; you are not ill? "

"Ill? No. "

"I have had a bad dream about you. How is it that I see you up and dressed? "

"My good fellow, I may as well ask you how it is that I see *you* up and undressed? "

"I have told you why. I have had a bad dream about you. I tried to rest after it, but it was impossible. I could not make up my mind to stay where I was without knowing you were safe; and yet I could not make up my mind to come in here. I have been minutes hesitating at the door. It is so easy to laugh at a dream that you have not dreamed. Where is your candle? "

"Burnt out. "

"I have a whole one in my room. Shall I fetch it? "

"Do so. "

His room was very near, and he was absent for but a few seconds. Coming back with the candle in his hand, he kneeled down on the hearth and lighted it. As he blew with his breath a charred billet into flame for the purpose, Vendale, looking down at him, saw that his lips were white and not easy of control.

"Yes! " said Obenreizer, setting the lighted candle on the table, "it was a bad dream. Only look at me! "

His feet were bare; his red-flannel shirt was thrown back at the throat, and its sleeves were rolled above the elbows; his only other garment, a pair of under pantaloons or drawers, reaching to the ankles, fitted him close and tight. A certain lithe and savage appearance was on his figure, and his eyes were very bright.

"If there had been a wrestle with a robber, as I dreamed, " said Obenreizer, "you see, I was stripped for it. "

"And armed too, " said Vendale, glancing at his girdle.

"A traveller's dagger, that I always carry on the road, " he answered carelessly, half drawing it from its sheath with his left hand, and putting it back again. "Do you carry no such thing? "

"Nothing of the kind. "

"No pistols? " said Obenreizer, glancing at the table, and from it to the untouched pillow.

"Nothing of the sort. "

"You Englishmen are so confident! You wish to sleep? "

"I have wished to sleep this long time, but I can't do it. "

"I neither, after the bad dream. My fire has gone the way of your candle. May I come and sit by yours? Two o'clock! It will so soon be four, that it is not worth the trouble to go to bed again. "

"I shall not take the trouble to go to bed at all, now, " said Vendale; "sit here and keep me company, and welcome. "

Going back to his room to arrange his dress, Obenreizer soon returned in a loose cloak and slippers, and they sat down on opposite sides of the hearth. In the interval Vendale had replenished the fire from the wood- basket in his room, and Obenreizer had put upon the table a flask and cup from his.

"Common cabaret brandy, I am afraid, " he said, pouring out; "bought upon the road, and not like yours from Cripple Corner. But yours is exhausted; so much the worse. A cold night, a cold time of night, a cold country, and a cold house. This may be better than nothing; try it. "

Vendale took the cup, and did so.

"How do you find it? "

"It has a coarse after-flavour, " said Vendale, giving back the cup with a slight shudder, "and I don't like it. "

"You are right, " said Obenreizer, tasting, and smacking his lips; "it *has* a coarse after-flavour, and *I* don't like it. Booh! It burns, though! " He had flung what remained in the cup upon the fire.

Each of them leaned an elbow on the table, reclined his head upon his hand, and sat looking at the flaring logs. Obenreizer remained watchful and still; but Vendale, after certain nervous twitches and starts, in one of which he rose to his feet and looked wildly about him, fell into the strangest confusion of dreams. He carried his papers in a leather case or pocket-book, in an inner breast-pocket of his buttoned travelling-coat; and whatever he dreamed of, in the lethargy that got possession of him, something importunate in those papers called him out of that dream, though he could not wake from it. He was berated on the steppes of Russia (some shadowy person gave that name to the place) with Marguerite; and yet the sensation of a hand at his breast, softly feeling the outline of the packet-book as he lay asleep before the fire, was present to him. He was ship-wrecked in an open boat at sea, and having lost his clothes, had no other covering than an old sail; and yet a creeping hand, tracing outside all the other pockets of the dress he actually wore, for papers, and finding none answer its touch, warned him to rouse himself. He was in the ancient vault at Cripple Corner, to which was transferred the very bed substantial and present in that very room at Basle; and Wilding (not dead, as he had supposed, and yet he did not wonder much) shook him, and whispered, "Look at that man! Don't you see he has risen, and is turning the pillow? Why should he turn the pillow, if not to seek those papers that are in your breast? Awake! " And yet he slept, and wandered off into other dreams.

Watchful and still, with his elbow on the table, and his head upon that hand, his companion at length said: "Vendale! We are called. Past Four! " Then, opening his eyes, he saw, turned sideways on him, the filmy face of Obenreizer.

"You have been in a heavy sleep, " he said. "The fatigue of constant travelling and the cold! "

"I am broad awake now, " cried Vendale, springing up, but with an unsteady footing. "Haven't you slept at all? "

"I may have dozed, but I seem to have been patiently looking at the fire. Whether or no, we must wash, and breakfast, and turn out. Past four, Vendale; past four! "

It was said in a tone to rouse him, for already he was half asleep again. In his preparation for the day, too, and at his breakfast, he was often virtually asleep while in mechanical action. It was not until the cold dark day was closing in, that he had any distincter impressions of the ride than jingling bells, bitter weather, slipping horses, frowning hill- sides, bleak woods, and a stoppage at some wayside house of entertainment, where they had passed through a cow-house to reach the travellers' room above. He had been conscious of little more, except of Obenreizer sitting thoughtful at his side all day, and eyeing him much.

But when he shook off his stupor, Obenreizer was not at his side. The carriage was stopping to bait at another wayside house; and a line of long narrow carts, laden with casks of wine, and drawn by horses with a quantity of blue collar and head-gear, were baiting too. These came from the direction in which the travellers were going, and Obenreizer (not thoughtful now, but cheerful and alert) was talking with the foremost driver. As Vendale stretched his limbs, circulated his blood, and cleared off the lees of his lethargy, with a sharp run to and fro in the bracing air, the line of carts moved on: the drivers all saluting Obenreizer as they passed him.

"Who are those? " asked Vendale.

"They are our carriers—Defresnier and Company's, " replied Obenreizer. "Those are our casks of wine. " He was singing to himself, and lighting a cigar.

"I have been drearily dull company to-day, " said Vendale. "I don't know what has been the matter with me. "

"You had no sleep last night; and a kind of brain-congestion frequently comes, at first, of such cold, " said Obenreizer. "I have seen it often. After all, we shall have our journey for nothing, it seems. "

"How for nothing? "

"The House is at Milan. You know, we are a Wine House at Neuchatel, and a Silk House at Milan? Well, Silk happening to press of a sudden, more than Wine, Defresnier was summoned to Milan. Rolland, the other partner, has been taken ill since his departure, and the doctors will allow him to see no one. A letter awaits you at Neuchatel to tell you so. I have it from our chief carrier whom you saw me talking with. He was surprised to see me, and said he had that word for you if he met you. What do you do? Go back? "

"Go on, " said Vendale.

"On? "

"On? Yes. Across the Alps, and down to Milan. "

Obenreizer stopped in his smoking to look at Vendale, and then smoked heavily, looked up the road, looked down the road, looked down at the stones in the road at his feet.

"I have a very serious matter in charge, " said Vendale; "more of these missing forms may be turned to as bad account, or worse: I am urged to lose no time in helping the House to take the thief; and nothing shall turn me back. "

"No? " cried Obenreizer, taking out his cigar to smile, and giving his hand to his fellow-traveller. "Then nothing shall turn *me* back. Ho, driver! Despatch. Quick there! Let us push on! "

They travelled through the night. There had been snow, and there was a partial thaw, and they mostly travelled at a foot-pace, and always with many stoppages to breathe the splashed and floundering horses. After an hour's broad daylight, they drew rein at the inn-door at Neuchatel, having been some eight-and-twenty hours in conquering some eighty English miles.

When they had hurriedly refreshed and changed, they went together to the house of business of Defresnier and Company. There they found the letter which the wine-carrier had described, enclosing the tests and comparisons of handwriting essential to the discovery of the Forger. Vendale's determination to press forward, without resting, being already taken, the only question to delay them was by what Pass could they cross the Alps? Respecting the state of the two Passes of the St. Gotthard and the Simplon, the guides and mule-drivers differed greatly; and both passes were still far enough off, to prevent the travellers from having the benefit of any recent experience of either. Besides which, they well knew that a fall of snow might altogether change the described conditions in a single hour, even if they were correctly stated. But, on the whole, the Simplon appearing to be the hopefuller route, Vendale decided to take it. Obenreizer bore little or no part in the discussion, and scarcely spoke.

To Geneva, to Lausanne, along the level margin of the lake to Vevay, so into the winding valley between the spurs of the mountains, and into the valley of the Rhone. The sound of the carriage-wheels, as they rattled on, through the day, through the night, became as the wheels of a great clock, recording the hours. No change of weather varied the journey, after it had hardened into a sullen frost. In a sombre-yellow sky, they saw the Alpine ranges; and they saw enough of snow on nearer and much lower hill-tops and hill-sides, to sully, by contrast, the purity of lake, torrent, and waterfall, and make the villages look discoloured and dirty. But no snow fell, nor was there any snow-drift on the road. The stalking along the valley of more or less of white mist, changing on their hair and dress into icicles, was the only variety between them and the gloomy sky. And still by day, and still by night, the wheels. And still they rolled, in the hearing of one of them, to the burden, altered from the burden of the Rhine: "The time is gone for robbing him alive, and I must murder him. "

They came, at length, to the poor little town of Brieg, at the foot of the Simplon. They came there after dark, but yet could see how dwarfed men's works and men became with the immense mountains towering over them. Here they must lie for the night; and here was warmth of fire, and lamp, and dinner, and wine, and after-conference resounding, with guides and drivers. No human creature had come across the Pass for four days. The snow above the snow-line was too soft for wheeled carriage, and not hard enough for sledge. There was snow in the sky. There had been snow in the sky for days past, and the marvel was that it had not fallen, and the certainty was that it must fall. No vehicle could cross. The journey might be tried on mules, or it might be tried on foot; but the best guides must be paid danger-price in either case, and that, too, whether they succeeded in taking the two travellers across, or turned for safety and brought them back.

In this discussion, Obenreizer bore no part whatever. He sat silently smoking by the fire until the room was cleared and Vendale referred to him.

"Bah! I am weary of these poor devils and their trade, " he said, in reply. "Always the same story. It is the story of their trade to-day, as it was the story of their trade when I was a ragged boy. What do you and I want? We want a knapsack each, and a mountain-staff each. We want no guide; we should guide him; he would not guide us. We leave our portmanteaus here, and we cross together. We have been on the mountains together before now, and I am mountain-born, and I know this Pass—Pass! —rather High Road! —by heart. We will leave these poor devils, in pity, to trade with others; but they must not delay us to make a pretence of earning money. Which is all they mean. "

Vendale, glad to be quit of the dispute, and to cut the knot: active, adventurous, bent on getting forward, and therefore very susceptible to the last hint: readily assented. Within two hours, they had purchased what they wanted for the expedition, had packed their knapsacks, and lay down to sleep.

At break of day, they found half the town collected in the narrow street to see them depart. The people talked together in groups; the guides and drivers whispered apart, and looked up at the sky; no one wished them a good journey.

As they began the ascent, a gleam of run shone from the otherwise unaltered sky, and for a moment turned the tin spires of the town to silver.

"A good omen! " said Vendale (though it died out while he spoke). "Perhaps our example will open the Pass on this side. "

"No; we shall not be followed, " returned Obenreizer, looking up at the sky and back at the valley. "We shall be alone up yonder. "

## ON THE MOUNTAIN

The road was fair enough for stout walkers, and the air grew lighter and easier to breathe as the two ascended. But the settled gloom remained as it had remained for days back. Nature seemed to have come to a pause. The sense of hearing, no less than the sense of sight, was troubled by having to wait so long for the change, whatever it might be, that impended. The silence was as palpable and heavy as the lowering clouds—or rather cloud, for there seemed to be but one in all the sky, and that one covering the whole of it.

Although the light was thus dismally shrouded, the prospect was not obscured. Down in the valley of the Rhone behind them, the stream could be traced through all its many windings, oppressively sombre and solemn in its one leaden hue, a colourless waste. Far and high above them, glaciers and suspended avalanches overhung the spots where they must pass, by-and-by; deep and dark below them on their right, were awful precipice and roaring torrent; tremendous mountains arose in every vista. The gigantic landscape, uncheered by a touch of changing light or a solitary ray of sun, was yet terribly distinct in its ferocity. The hearts of two lonely men might shrink a little, if they had to win their way for miles and hours among a legion of silent and motionless men—mere men like themselves—all looking at them with fixed and frowning front. But how much more, when the legion is of Nature's mightiest works, and the frown may turn to fury in an instant!

As they ascended, the road became gradually more rugged and difficult. But the spirits of Vendale rose as they mounted higher, leaving so much more of the road behind them conquered. Obenreizer spoke little, and held on with a determined purpose. Both, in respect of agility and endurance, were well qualified for the expedition. Whatever the born mountaineer read in the weather-tokens that was illegible to the other, he kept to himself.

"Shall we get across to-day? " asked Vendale.

"No, " replied the other. "You see how much deeper the snow lies here than it lay half a league lower. The higher we mount the deeper the snow will lie. Walking is half wading even now. And the days are so short! If we get as high as the fifth Refuge, and lie to-night at the Hospice, we shall do well. "

"Is there no danger of the weather rising in the night, " asked Vendale, anxiously, "and snowing us up? "

"There is danger enough about us, " said Obenreizer, with a cautious glance onward and upward, "to render silence our best policy. You have heard of the Bridge of the Ganther? "

"I have crossed it once. "

"In the summer? "

"Yes; in the travelling season. "

"Yes; but it is another thing at this season; " with a sneer, as though he were out of temper. "This is not a time of year, or a state of things, on an Alpine Pass, that you gentlemen holiday-travellers know much about. "

"You are my Guide, " said Vendale, good humouredly. "I trust to you. "

"I am your Guide, " said Obenreizer, "and I will guide you to your journey's end. There is the Bridge before us. "

They had made a turn into a desolate and dismal ravine, where the snow lay deep below them, deep above them, deep on every side. While speaking, Obenreizer stood pointing at the Bridge, and observing Vendale's face, with a very singular expression on his own.

"If I, as Guide, had sent you over there, in advance, and encouraged you to give a shout or two, you might have brought down upon yourself tons and tons and tons of snow, that would not only have struck you dead, but buried you deep, at a blow. "

"No doubt, " said Vendale.

"No doubt. But that is not what I have to do, as Guide. So pass silently. Or, going as we go, our indiscretion might else crush and bury *me*. Let us get on! "

There was a great accumulation of snow on the Bridge; and such enormous accumulations of snow overhung them from protecting masses of rock, that they might have been making their way through a stormy sky of white clouds. Using his staff skilfully, sounding as he went, and looking upward, with bent shoulders, as it were to resist the mere idea of a fall from above, Obenreizer softly led. Vendale closely followed. They were yet in the midst of their dangerous way, when there came a mighty rush, followed by a sound as of thunder. Obenreizer clapped his hand on Vendale's mouth and pointed to the track behind them. Its aspect had been wholly changed in a moment. An avalanche had swept over it, and plunged into the torrent at the bottom of the gulf below.

Their appearance at the solitary Inn not far beyond this terrible Bridge, elicited many expressions of astonishment from the people shut up in the house. "We stay but to rest, " said Obenreizer, shaking the snow from his dress at the fire. "This gentleman has very pressing occasion to get across; tell them, Vendale. "

"Assuredly, I have very pressing occasion. I must cross. "

"You hear, all of you. My friend has very pressing occasion to get across, and we want no advice and no help. I am as good a guide, my fellow-countrymen, as any of you. Now, give us to eat and drink. "

In exactly the same way, and in nearly the same words, when it was coming on dark and they had struggled through the greatly increased difficulties of the road, and had at last reached their destination for the night, Obenreizer said to the astonished people of the Hospice, gathering about them at the fire, while they were yet in the act of getting their wet shoes off, and shaking the snow from their clothes:

"It is well to understand one another, friends all. This gentleman —"

"—Has, " said Vendale, readily taking him up with a smile, "very pressing occasion to get across. Must cross. "

"You hear? —has very pressing occasion to get across, must cross. We want no advice and no help. I am mountain-born, and act as Guide. Do not worry us by talking about it, but let us have supper, and wine, and bed. "

All through the intense cold of the night, the same awful stillness. Again at sunrise, no sunny tinge to gild or redden the snow. The same interminable waste of deathly white; the same immovable air; the same monotonous gloom in the sky.

"Travellers! " a friendly voice called to them from the door, after they were afoot, knapsack on back and staff in hand, as yesterday; "recollect! There are five places of shelter, near together, on the dangerous road before you; and there is the wooden cross, and there is the next Hospice. Do not stray from the track. If the *Tourmente* comes on, take shelter instantly! "

"The trade of these poor devils! " said Obenreizer to his friend, with a contemptuous backward wave of his hand towards the voice. "How they stick to their trade! You Englishmen say we Swiss are mercenary. Truly, it does look like it. "

They had divided between the two knapsacks such refreshments as they had been able to obtain that morning, and as they deemed it prudent to take. Obenreizer carried the wine as his share of the burden; Vendale, the bread and meat and cheese, and the flask of brandy.

They had for some time laboured upward and onward through the snow — which was now above their knees in the track, and of unknown depth elsewhere—and they were still labouring upward and onward through the most frightful part of that tremendous desolation, when snow begin to fall. At first, but a few flakes descended slowly and steadily. After a little while the fall grew much denser, and suddenly it began without apparent cause to whirl itself into spiral shapes. Instantly ensuing upon this last change, an icy blast came roaring at them, and every sound and force imprisoned until now was let loose.

One of the dismal galleries through which the road is carried at that perilous point, a cave eked out by arches of great strength, was near at hand. They struggled into it, and the storm raged wildly. The noise of the wind, the noise of the water, the thundering down of displaced masses of rock and snow, the awful voices with which not only that gorge but every gorge in the whole monstrous range seemed to be suddenly endowed, the darkness as of night, the violent revolving of the snow which beat and broke it into spray and blinded them, the madness of everything around insatiate for destruction, the rapid substitution of furious violence for unnatural calm, and hosts of appalling sounds for silence: these were things, on the edge of a deep abyss, to chill the blood, though the fierce wind, made actually solid by ice and snow, had failed to chill it.

Obenreizer, walking to and fro in the gallery without ceasing, signed to Vendale to help him unbuckle his knapsack. They could see each other, but could not have heard each other speak. Vendale complying, Obenreizer produced his bottle of wine, and poured some out, motioning Vendale to take that for warmth's sake, and not brandy. Vendale again complying, Obenreizer seemed to drink after him, and the two walked backwards and forwards side by side; both well knowing that to rest or sleep would be to die.

The snow came driving heavily into the gallery by the upper end at which they would pass out of it, if they ever passed out; for greater dangers lay on the road behind them than before. The snow soon began to choke the arch. An hour more, and it lay so high as to block out half the returning daylight. But it froze hard now, as it fell, and could be clambered through or over. The violence of the mountain storm was gradually yielding to steady snowfall. The wind still raged at intervals, but not incessantly; and when it paused, the snow fell in heavy flakes.

They might have been two hours in their frightful prison, when Obenreizer, now crunching into the mound, now creeping over it with his head bowed down and his body touching the top of the arch, made his way out. Vendale followed close upon him, but followed without clear motive or calculation. For the lethargy of Basle was creeping over him again, and mastering his senses.

How far he had followed out of the gallery, or with what obstacles he had since contended, he knew not. He became roused to the knowledge that Obenreizer had set upon him, and that they were struggling desperately in the snow. He became roused to the remembrance of what his assailant carried in a girdle. He felt for it, drew it, struck at him, struggled again, struck at him again, cast him off, and stood face to face with him.

"I promised to guide you to your journey's end, " said Obenreizer, "and I have kept my promise. The journey of your life ends here. Nothing can prolong it. You are sleeping as you stand. "

"You are a villain. What have you done to me? "

"You are a fool. I have drugged you. You are doubly a fool, for I drugged you once before upon the journey, to try you. You are trebly a fool, for I am the thief and forger, and in a few moments I shall take those proofs against the thief and forger from your insensible body. "

The entrapped man tried to throw off the lethargy, but its fatal hold upon him was so sure that, even while he heard those words, he stupidly wondered which of them had been wounded, and whose blood it was that he saw sprinkled on the snow.

"What have I done to you, " he asked, heavily and thickly, "that you should be—so base—a murderer? "

"Done to me? You would have destroyed me, but that you have come to your journey's end. Your cursed activity interposed between me, and the time I had counted on in which I might have replaced the money. Done to me? You have come in my way—not once, not twice, but again and again and again. Did I try to shake you off in the beginning, or no? You were not to be shaken off. Therefore you die here. "

Vendale tried to think coherently, tried to speak coherently, tried to pick up the iron-shod staff he had let fall; failing to touch it, tried to stagger on without its aid. All in vain, all in vain! He stumbled, and fell heavily forward on the brink of the deep chasm.

Stupefied, dozing, unable to stand upon his feet, a veil before his eyes, his sense of hearing deadened, he made such a vigorous rally that, supporting himself on his hands, he saw his enemy standing calmly over him, and heard him speak. "You call me murderer, " said Obenreizer, with a grim laugh. "The name matters very little. But at least I have set my life against yours, for I am surrounded by dangers, and may never make my way out of this place. The *Tourmente* is rising again. The snow is on the whirl. I must have the papers now. Every moment has my life in it. "

"Stop! " cried Vendale, in a terrible voice, staggering up with a last flash of fire breaking out of him, and clutching the thievish hands at his breast, in both of his. "Stop! Stand away from me! God bless my Marguerite! Happily she will never know how I died. Stand off from me, and let me look at your murderous face. Let it remind me—of something—left to say. "

The sight of him fighting so hard for his senses, and the doubt whether he might not for the instant be possessed by the strength of a dozen men, kept his opponent still. Wildly glaring at him, Vendale faltered out the broken words:

"It shall not be—the trust—of the dead—betrayed by me—reputed parents—misinherited fortune—see to it! "

As his head dropped on his breast, and he stumbled on the brink of the chasm as before, the thievish hands went once more, quick and busy, to his breast. He made a convulsive attempt to cry "No! " desperately rolled himself over into the gulf; and sank away from his enemy's touch, like a phantom in a dreadful dream.

\* \* \* \* \*

The mountain storm raged again, and passed again. The awful mountain- voices died away, the moon rose, and the soft and silent snow fell.

Two men and two large dogs came out at the door of the Hospice. The men looked carefully around them, and up at the sky. The dogs rolled in the snow, and took it into their mouths, and cast it up with their paws.

One of the men said to the other: "We may venture now. We may find them in one of the five Refuges. " Each fastened on his back a basket; each took in his hand a strong spiked pole; each girded under his arms a looped end of a stout rope, so that they were tied together.

Suddenly the dogs desisted from their gambols in the snow, stood looking down the ascent, put their noses up, put their noses down, became greatly excited, and broke into a deep loud bay together.

The two men looked in the faces of the two dogs. The two dogs looked, with at least equal intelligence, in the faces of the two men.

"Au secours, then! Help! To the rescue! " cried the two men. The two dogs, with a glad, deep, generous bark, bounded away.

"Two more mad ones! " said the men, stricken motionless, and looking away in the moonlight. "Is it possible in such weather! And one of them a woman! "

Each of the dogs had the corner of a woman's dress in its mouth, and drew her along. She fondled their heads as she came up, and she came up through the snow with an accustomed tread. Not so the large man with her, who was spent and winded.

"Dear guides, dear friends of travellers! I am of your country. We seek two gentlemen crossing the Pass, who should have reached the Hospice this evening. "

"They have reached it, ma'amselle. "

"Thank Heaven! O thank Heaven! "

"But, unhappily, they have gone on again. We are setting forth to seek them even now. We had to wait until the *Tourmente* passed. It has been fearful up here. "

"Dear guides, dear friends of travellers! Let me go with you. Let me go with you for the love of GOD! One of those gentlemen is to be my husband. I love him, O, so dearly. O so dearly! You see I am not faint, you see I am not tired. I am born a peasant girl. I will show you that I know well how to fasten myself to your ropes. I will do it with my own hands. I will swear to be brave and good. But let me go with you, let me go with you! If any mischance should have befallen him, my love would find him, when nothing else could. On my knees, dear friends of travellers! By the love your dear mothers had for your fathers! "

The good rough fellows were moved. "After all, " they murmured to one another, "she speaks but the truth. She knows the ways of the mountains. See how marvellously she has come here. But as to Monsieur there, ma'amselle? "

"Dear Mr. Joey, " said Marguerite, addressing him in his own tongue, "you will remain at the house, and wait for me; will you not? "

"If I know'd which o' you two recommended it, " growled Joey Ladle, eyeing the two men with great indignation, "I'd fight you for sixpence, and give you half-a-crown towards your expenses. No, Miss. I'll stick by you as long as there's any sticking left in me, and I'll die for you when I can't do better. "

The state of the moon rendering it highly important that no time should be lost, and the dogs showing signs of great uneasiness, the two men quickly took their resolution. The rope that yoked them together was exchanged for a longer one; the party were secured, Marguerite second, and the Cellarman last; and they set out for the Refuges. The actual distance of those places was nothing: the whole five, and the next Hospice to boot, being within two miles; but the ghastly way was whitened out and sheeted over.

They made no miss in reaching the Gallery where the two had taken shelter. The second storm of wind and snow had so wildly swept over it since, that their tracks were gone. But the dogs went to and fro with their noses down, and were confident. The party stopping, however, at the further arch, where the second storm had been especially furious, and where the drift was deep, the dogs became troubled, and went about and about, in quest of a lost purpose.

The great abyss being known to lie on the right, they wandered too much to the left, and had to regain the way with infinite labour through a deep field of snow. The leader of the line had stopped it, and was taking note of the landmarks, when one of the dogs fell to tearing up the snow a little before them. Advancing and stooping to look at it, thinking that some one might be overwhelmed there, they saw that it was stained, and that the stain was red.

The other dog was now seen to look over the brink of the gulf, with his fore legs straightened out, lest he should fall into it, and to tremble in every limb. Then the dog who had found the stained snow joined him, and then they ran to and fro, distressed and whining. Finally, they both stopped on the brink together, and setting up their heads, howled dolefully.

"There is some one lying below, " said Marguerite.

"I think so, " said the foremost man. "Stand well inward, the two last, and let us look over. "

The last man kindled two torches from his basket, and handed them forward. The leader taking one, and Marguerite the other, they looked down; now shading the torches, now moving them to the right or left, now raising them, now depressing them, as moonlight far below contended with black shadows. A piercing cry from Marguerite broke a long silence.

"My God! On a projecting point, where a wall of ice stretches forward over the torrent, I see a human form! "

"Where, ma'amselle, where? "

"See, there! On the shelf of ice below the dogs! "

The leader, with a sickened aspect, drew inward, and they were all silent. But they were not all inactive, for Marguerite, with swift and skilful fingers, had detached both herself and him from the rope in a few seconds.

"Show me the baskets. These two are the only ropes? "

"The only ropes here, ma'amselle; but at the Hospice —"

"If he is alive—I know it is my lover—he will be dead before you can return. Dear Guides! Blessed friends of travellers! Look at me. Watch my hands. If they falter or go wrong, make me your prisoner by force. If they are steady and go right, help me to save him! "

She girded herself with a cord under the breast and arms, she formed it into a kind of jacket, she drew it into knots, she laid its end side by side with the end of the other cord, she twisted and twined the two together, she knotted them together, she set her foot upon the knots, she strained them, she held them for the two men to strain at.

"She is inspired, " they said to one another.

"By the Almighty's mercy! " she exclaimed. "You both know that I am by far the lightest here. Give me the brandy and the wine, and lower me down to him. Then go for assistance and a stronger rope. You see that when it is lowered to me—look at this about me now—I can make it fast and safe to his body. Alive or dead, I will bring him up, or die with him. I love him passionately. Can I say more? "

They turned to her companion, but he was lying senseless on the snow.

"Lower me down to him, " she said, taking two little kegs they had brought, and hanging them about her, "or I will dash myself to pieces! I am a peasant, and I know no giddiness or fear; and this is nothing to me, and I passionately love him. Lower me down! "

"Ma'amselle, ma'amselle, he must be dying or dead. "

"Dying or dead, my husband's head shall lie upon my breast, or I will dash myself to pieces. "

They yielded, overborne. With such precautions as their skill and the circumstances admitted, they let her slip from the summit, guiding herself down the precipitous icy wall with her hand, and they lowered down, and lowered down, and lowered down, until the cry came up: "Enough! "

"Is it really he, and is he dead? " they called down, looking over.

The cry came up: "He is insensible; but his heart beats. It beats against mine. "

"How does he lie? "

The cry came up: "Upon a ledge of ice. It has thawed beneath him, and it will thaw beneath me. Hasten. If we die, I am content. "

One of the two men hurried off with the dogs at such topmost speed as he could make; the other set up the lighted torches in the snow, and applied himself to recovering the Englishman. Much snow-chafing and some brandy got him on his legs, but delirious and quite unconscious where he was.

The watch remained upon the brink, and his cry went down continually: "Courage! They will soon be here. How goes it? " And the cry came up: "His heart still beats against mine. I warm him in my arms. I have cast off the rope, for the ice melts under us, and the rope would separate me from him; but I am not afraid. "

The moon went down behind the mountain tops, and all the abyss lay in darkness. The cry went down: "How goes it? " The cry came up: "We are sinking lower, but his heart still beats against mine. "

At length the eager barking of the dogs, and a flare of light upon the snow, proclaimed that help was coming on. Twenty or thirty men, lamps, torches, litters, ropes, blankets, wood to kindle a great fire, restoratives and stimulants, came in fast. The dogs ran from one man to another, and from this thing to that, and ran to the edge of the abyss, dumbly entreating Speed, speed, speed!

The cry went down: "Thanks to God, all is ready. How goes it? "

The cry came up: "We are sinking still, and we are deadly cold. His heart no longer beats against mine. Let no one come down, to add to our weight. Lower the rope only. "

The fire was kindled high, a great glare of torches lighted the sides of the precipice, lamps were lowered, a strong rope was lowered. She could be seen passing it round him, and making it secure.

The cry came up into a deathly silence: "Raise! Softly! " They could see her diminished figure shrink, as he was swung into the air.

They gave no shout when some of them laid him on a litter, and others lowered another strong rope. The cry again came up into a deathly silence: "Raise! Softly! " But when they caught her at the brink, then they shouted, then they wept, then they gave thanks to Heaven, then they kissed her feet, then they kissed her dress, then the dogs caressed her, licked her icy hands, and with their honest faces warmed her frozen bosom!

She broke from them all, and sank over him on his litter, with both her loving hands upon the heart that stood still.

## ACT IV.

## THE CLOCK-LOCK

The pleasant scene was Neuchatel; the pleasant month was April; the pleasant place was a notary's office; the pleasant person in it was the notary: a rosy, hearty, handsome old man, chief notary of Neuchatel, known far and wide in the canton as Maitre Voigt. Professionally and personally, the notary was a popular citizen. His innumerable kindnesses and his innumerable oddities had for years made him one of the recognised public characters of the pleasant Swiss town. His long brown frock-coat and his black skull-cap, were among the institutions of the place: and he carried a snuff-box which, in point of size, was popularly believed to be without a parallel in Europe.

There was another person in the notary's office, not so pleasant as the notary. This was Obenreizer.

An oddly pastoral kind of office it was, and one that would never have answered in England. It stood in a neat back yard, fenced off from a pretty flower-garden. Goats browsed in the doorway, and a cow was within half-a-dozen feet of keeping company with the clerk. Maitre Voigt's room was a bright and varnished little room, with panelled walls, like a toy- chamber. According to the seasons of the year, roses, sunflowers, hollyhocks, peeped in at the windows. Maitre Voigt's bees hummed through the office all the summer, in at this window and out at that, taking it frequently in their day's work, as if honey were to be made from Maitre Voigt's sweet disposition. A large musical box on the chimney-piece often trilled away at the Overture to Fra Diavolo, or a Selection from William Tell, with a chirruping liveliness that had to be stopped by force on the entrance of a client, and irrepressibly broke out again the moment his back was turned.

"Courage, courage, my good fellow! " said Maitre Voigt, patting Obenreizer on the knee, in a fatherly and comforting way. "You will begin a new life to-morrow morning in my office here. "

Obenreizer—dressed in mourning, and subdued in manner—lifted his hand, with a white handkerchief in it, to the region of his heart. "The gratitude is here, " he said. "But the words to express it are not here. "

"Ta-ta-ta! Don't talk to me about gratitude! " said Maitre Voigt. "I hate to see a man oppressed. I see you oppressed, and I hold out my hand to you by instinct. Besides, I am not too old yet, to remember my young days. Your father sent me my first client. (It was on a question of half an acre of vineyard that seldom bore any grapes. ) Do I owe nothing to your father's son? I owe him a debt of friendly obligation, and I pay it to you. That's rather neatly expressed, I think, " added Maitre Voigt, in high good humour with himself. "Permit me to reward my own merit with a pinch of snuff! "

Obenreizer dropped his eyes to the ground, as though he were not even worthy to see the notary take snuff.

"Do me one last favour, sir, " he said, when he raised his eyes. "Do not act on impulse. Thus far, you have only a general knowledge of my position. Hear the case for and against me, in its details, before you take me into your office. Let my claim on your benevolence be recognised by your sound reason as well as by your excellent heart. In *that* case, I may hold up my head against the bitterest of my enemies, and build myself a new reputation on the ruins of the character I have lost. "

"As you will, " said Maitre Voigt. "You speak well, my son. You will be a fine lawyer one of these days. "

"The details are not many, " pursued Obenreizer. "My troubles begin with the accidental death of my late travelling companion, my lost dear friend Mr. Vendale. "

"Mr. Vendale, " repeated the notary. "Just so. I have heard and read of the name, several times within these two months. The name of the unfortunate English gentleman who was killed on the Simplon. When you got that scar upon your cheek and neck. "

"—From my own knife, " said Obenreizer, touching what must have been an ugly gash at the time of its infliction.

"From your own knife, " assented the notary, "and in trying to save him. Good, good, good. That was very good. Vendale. Yes. I have several times, lately, thought it droll that I should once have had a client of that name. "

"But the world, sir, " returned Obenreizer, "is *so* small! " Nevertheless he made a mental note that the notary had once had a client of that name.

"As I was saying, sir, the death of that dear travelling comrade begins my troubles. What follows? I save myself. I go down to Milan. I am received with coldness by Defresnier and Company. Shortly afterwards, I am discharged by Defresnier and Company. Why? They give no reason why. I ask, do they assail my honour? No answer. I ask, what is the imputation against me? No answer. I ask, where are their proofs against me? No answer. I ask, what am I to think? The reply is, 'M. Obenreizer is free to think what he will. What M. Obenreizer thinks, is of no importance to Defresnier and Company. ' And that is all. "

"Perfectly. That is all, " asserted the notary, taking a large pinch of snuff.

"But is that enough, sir? "

"That is not enough, " said Maitre Voigt. "The House of Defresnier are my fellow townsmen — much respected, much esteemed — but the House of Defresnier must not silently destroy a man's character. You can rebut assertion. But how can you rebut silence? "

"Your sense of justice, my dear patron, " answered Obenreizer, "states in a word the cruelty of the case. Does it stop there? No. For, what follows upon that? "

"True, my poor boy, " said the notary, with a comforting nod or two; "your ward rebels upon that. "

"Rebels is too soft a word, " retorted Obenreizer. "My ward revolts from me with horror. My ward defies me. My ward withdraws herself from my authority, and takes shelter (Madame Dor with her) in the house of that English lawyer, Mr. Bintrey, who replies to your summons to her to submit herself to my authority, that she will not do so. "

" — And who afterwards writes, " said the notary, moving his large snuff- box to look among the papers underneath it for the letter, "that he is coming to confer with me. "

"Indeed? " replied Obenreizer, rather checked. "Well, sir. Have I no legal rights? "

"Assuredly, my poor boy, " returned the notary. "All but felons have their legal rights. "

"And who calls me felon? " said Obenreizer, fiercely.

"No one. Be calm under your wrongs. If the House of Defresnier would call you felon, indeed, we should know how to deal with them. "

While saying these words, he had handed Bintrey's very short letter to Obenreizer, who now read it and gave it back.

"In saying, " observed Obenreizer, with recovered composure, "that he is coming to confer with you, this English lawyer means that he is coming to deny my authority over my ward. "

"You think so? "

"I am sure of it. I know him. He is obstinate and contentious. You will tell me, my dear sir, whether my authority is unassailable, until my ward is of age? "

"Absolutely unassailable. "

"I will enforce it. I will make her submit herself to it. For, " said Obenreizer, changing his angry tone to one of grateful submission, "I owe it to you, sir; to you, who have so confidingly taken an injured man under your protection, and into your employment. "

"Make your mind easy, " said Maitre Voigt. "No more of this now, and no thanks! Be here to-morrow morning, before the other clerk comes—between seven and eight. You will find me in this room; and I will myself initiate you in your work. Go away! go away! I have letters to write. I won't hear a word more. "

Dismissed with this generous abruptness, and satisfied with the favourable impression he had left on the old man's mind, Obenreizer was at leisure to revert to the mental note he had made that Maitre Voigt once had a client whose name was Vendale.

"I ought to know England well enough by this time; " so his meditations ran, as he sat on a bench in the yard; "and it is not a name I ever encountered there, except—" he looked involuntarily over his shoulder—"as *his* name. Is the world so small that I cannot get away from him, even now when he is dead? He confessed at the last that he had betrayed the trust of the dead, and misinherited a fortune. And I was to see to it. And I was to stand off, that my face might remind him of it. Why *my* face, unless it concerned *me*? I am sure of his words, for they have been in my ears ever since. Can there be anything bearing on them, in the keeping of this old idiot? Anything to repair my fortunes, and blacken his memory? He dwelt upon my earliest remembrances, that night at Basle. Why, unless he had a purpose in it? "

Maitre Voigt's two largest he-goats were butting at him to butt him out of the place, as if for that disrespectful mention of their master. So he got up and left the place. But he walked alone for a long time on the border of the lake, with his head drooped in deep thought.

Between seven and eight next morning, he presented himself again at the office. He found the notary ready for him, at work on some papers which had come in on the previous evening. In a few clear words, Maitre Voigt explained the routine of the office, and the duties Obenreizer would be expected to perform. It still wanted five minutes to eight, when the preliminary instructions were declared to be complete.

"I will show you over the house and the offices, " said Maitre Voigt, "but I must put away these papers first. They come from the municipal authorities, and they must be taken special care of. "

Obenreizer saw his chance, here, of finding out the repository in which his employer's private papers were kept.

"Can't I save you the trouble, sir? " he asked. "Can't I put those documents away under your directions? "

Maitre Voigt laughed softly to himself; closed the portfolio in which the papers had been sent to him; handed it to Obenreizer.

"Suppose you try, " he said. "All my papers of importance are kept yonder. "

He pointed to a heavy oaken door, thickly studded with nails, at the lower end of the room. Approaching the door, with the portfolio, Obenreizer discovered, to his astonishment, that there were no means whatever of opening it from the outside. There was no handle, no bolt, no key, and (climax of passive obstruction! ) no keyhole.

"There is a second door to this room? " said Obenreizer, appealing to the notary.

"No, " said Maitre Voigt. "Guess again. "

"There is a window? "

"Nothing of the sort. The window has been bricked up. The only way in, is the way by that door. Do you give it up? " cried Maitre Voigt, in high triumph. "Listen, my good fellow, and tell me if you hear nothing inside? "

Obenreizer listened for a moment, and started back from the door.

"I know! " he exclaimed. "I heard of this when I was apprenticed here at the watchmaker's. Perrin Brothers have finished their famous clock-lock at last—and you have got it? "

"Bravo! " said Maitre Voigt. "The clock-lock it is! There, my son! There you have one more of what the good people of this town call, 'Daddy Voigt's follies. ' With all my heart! Let those laugh who win. No thief can steal *my* keys. No burglar can pick *my* lock. No power on earth, short of a battering-ram or a barrel of gunpowder, can move that door, till my little sentinel inside—my worthy friend who goes 'Tick, Tick, ' as I tell him—says, 'Open! ' The big door obeys the little Tick, Tick, and the little Tick, Tick, obeys *me*. That! " cried Daddy Voigt, snapping his fingers, "for all the thieves in Christendom! "

"May I see it in action? " asked Obenreizer. "Pardon my curiosity, dear sir! You know that I was once a tolerable worker in the clock trade. "

"Certainly you shall see it in action, " said Maitre Voigt. "What is the time now? One minute to eight. Watch, and in one minute you will see the door open of itself. "

In one minute, smoothly and slowly and silently, as if invisible hands had set it free, the heavy door opened inward, and disclosed a dark chamber beyond. On three sides, shelves filled the walls, from floor to ceiling. Arranged on the shelves, were rows upon rows of boxes made in the pretty inlaid woodwork of Switzerland, and bearing inscribed on their fronts (for the most part in fanciful coloured letters) the names of the notary's clients.

Maitre Voigt lighted a taper, and led the way into the room.

"You shall see the clock, " he said proudly. "I possess the greatest curiosity in Europe. It is only a privileged few whose eyes can look at it. I give the privilege to your good father's son—you shall be one of the favoured few who enter the room with me. See! here it is, on the right-hand wall at the side of the door. "

"An ordinary clock, " exclaimed Obenreizer. "No! Not an ordinary clock. It has only one hand. "

"Aha! " said Maitre Voigt. "Not an ordinary clock, my friend. No, no. That one hand goes round the dial. As I put it, so it regulates the hour at which the door shall open. See! The hand points to eight. At eight the door opened, as you saw for yourself. "

"Does it open more than once in the four-and-twenty hours? " asked Obenreizer.

"More than once? " repeated the notary, with great scorn. "You don't know my good friend, Tick-Tick! He will open the door as often as I ask him. All he wants is his directions, and he gets them here. Look below the dial. Here is a half-circle of steel let into the wall, and here is a hand (called the regulator) that travels round it, just as *my* hand chooses. Notice, if you please, that there are figures to guide me on the half-circle of steel. Figure I. means: Open once in the four-and-twenty hours. Figure II. means: Open twice; and so on to the end. I set the regulator every morning, after I have read my letters, and when I know what my day's work is to be. Would you like to see me set it now? What is to-day? Wednesday. Good! This is the day of our rifle-club; there is little business to do; I grant a half-holiday. No work here to- day, after three o'clock. Let us first put away this portfolio of municipal papers. There! No need to trouble Tick-Tick to open the door until eight to-morrow. Good! I leave the dial-hand at eight; I put back the regulator to I. ; I close the door; and closed the door remains, past all opening by anybody, till to-morrow morning at eight. "

Obenreizer's quickness instantly saw the means by which he might make the clock-lock betray its master's confidence, and place its master's papers at his disposal.

"Stop, sir! " he cried, at the moment when the notary was closing the door. "Don't I see something moving among the boxes—on the floor there? "

(Maitre Voigt turned his back for a moment to look. In that moment, Obenreizer's ready hand put the regulator on, from the figure "I. " to the figure "II. " Unless the notary looked again at the half-circle of steel, the door would open at eight that evening, as well as at eight next morning, and nobody but Obenreizer would know it. )

"There is nothing! " said Maitre Voigt. "Your troubles have shaken your nerves, my son. Some shadow thrown by my taper; or some poor little beetle, who lives among the old lawyer's secrets, running away from the light. Hark! I hear your fellow-clerk in the office. To work! to work! and build to-day the first step that leads to your new fortunes! "

He good-humouredly pushed Obenreizer out before him; extinguished the taper, with a last fond glance at his clock which passed harmlessly over the regulator beneath; and closed the oaken door.

At three, the office was shut up. The notary and everybody in the notary's employment, with one exception, went to see the rifle-shooting. Obenreizer had pleaded that he was not in spirits for a public festival. Nobody knew what had become of him. It was believed that he had slipped away for a solitary walk.

The house and offices had been closed but a few minutes, when the door of a shining wardrobe in the notary's shining room opened, and Obenreizer stopped out. He walked to a window, unclosed the shutters, satisfied himself that he could escape unseen by way of the garden, turned back into the room, and took his place in the notary's easy-chair. He was locked up in the house, and there were five hours to wait before eight o'clock came.

He wore his way through the five hours: sometimes reading the books and newspapers that lay on the table: sometimes thinking: sometimes walking to and fro. Sunset came on. He closed the window-shutters before he kindled a light. The candle lighted, and the time drawing nearer and nearer, he sat, watch in hand, with his eyes on the oaken door.

At eight, smoothly and softly and silently the door opened.

One after another, he read the names on the outer rows of boxes. No such name as Vendale! He removed the outer row, and looked at the row behind. These were older boxes, and shabbier boxes. The four first that he examined, were inscribed with French and German names. The fifth bore a name which was almost illegible. He brought it out into the room, and examined it closely. There, covered thickly with time-stains and dust, was the name: "Vendale. "

The key hung to the box by a string. He unlocked the box, took out four loose papers that were in it, spread them open on the table, and began to read them. He had not so occupied a minute, when his face fell from its expression of eagerness and avidity, to one of haggard astonishment and disappointment. But, after a little consideration, he copied the papers. He then replaced the papers, replaced the box, closed the door, extinguished the candle, and stole away.

As his murderous and thievish footfall passed out of the garden, the steps of the notary and some one accompanying him stopped at the front door of the house. The lamps were lighted in the little street, and the notary had his door-key in his hand.

"Pray do not pass my house, Mr. Bintrey, " he said. "Do me the honour to come in. It is one of our town half-holidays—our Tir—but my people will be back directly. It is droll that you should ask your way to the Hotel of me. Let us eat and drink before you go there. "

"Thank you; not to-night, " said Bintrey. "Shall I come to you at ten to- morrow? "

"I shall be enchanted, sir, to take so early an opportunity of redressing the wrongs of my injured client, " returned the good notary.

"Yes, " retorted Bintrey; "your injured client is all very well—but—a word in your ear. "

He whispered to the notary and walked off. When the notary's housekeeper came home, she found him standing at his door motionless, with the key still in his hand, and the door unopened.

## OBENREIZER'S VICTORY

The scene shifts again—to the foot of the Simplon, on the Swiss side.

In one of the dreary rooms of the dreary little inn at Brieg, Mr. Bintrey and Maitre Voigt sat together at a professional council of two. Mr. Bintrey was searching in his despatch-box. Maitre Voigt was looking towards a closed door, painted brown to imitate mahogany, and communicating with an inner room.

"Isn't it time he was here? " asked the notary, shifting his position, and glancing at a second door at the other end of the room, painted yellow to imitate deal.

"He *is* here, " answered Bintrey, after listening for a moment.

The yellow door was opened by a waiter, and Obenreizer walked in.

After greeting Maitre Voigt with a cordiality which appeared to cause the notary no little embarrassment, Obenreizer bowed with grave and distant politeness to Bintrey. "For what reason have I been brought from Neuchatel to the foot of the mountain? " he inquired, taking the seat which the English lawyer had indicated to him.

"You shall be quite satisfied on that head before our interview is over, " returned Bintrey. "For the present, permit me to suggest proceeding at once to business. There has been a correspondence, Mr. Obenreizer, between you and your niece. I am here to represent your niece. "

"In other words, you, a lawyer, are here to represent an infraction of the law. "

"Admirably put! " said Bintrey. "If all the people I have to deal with were only like you, what an easy profession mine would be! I am here to represent an infraction of the law—that is your point of view.

I am here to make a compromise between you and your niece — that is my point of view. "

"There must be two parties to a compromise, " rejoined Obenreizer. "I decline, in this case, to be one of them. The law gives me authority to control my niece's actions, until she comes of age. She is not yet of age; and I claim my authority. "

At this point Maitre attempted to speak. Bintrey silenced him with a compassionate indulgence of tone and manner, as if he was silencing a favourite child.

"No, my worthy friend, not a word. Don't excite yourself unnecessarily; leave it to me. " He turned, and addressed himself again to Obenreizer. "I can think of nothing comparable to you, Mr. Obenreizer, but granite — and even that wears out in course of time. In the interests of peace and quietness — for the sake of your own dignity — relax a little. If you will only delegate your authority to another person whom I know of, that person may be trusted never to lose sight of your niece, night or day! "

"You are wasting your time and mine, " returned Obenreizer. "If my niece is not rendered up to my authority within one week from this day, I invoke the law. If you resist the law, I take her by force. "

He rose to his feet as he said the last word. Maitre Voigt looked round again towards the brown door which led into the inner room.

"Have some pity on the poor girl, " pleaded Bintrey. "Remember how lately she lost her lover by a dreadful death! Will nothing move you? "

"Nothing. "

Bintrey, in his turn, rose to his feet, and looked at Maitre Voigt. Maitre Voigt's hand, resting on the table, began to tremble. Maitre Voigt's eyes remained fixed, as if by irresistible fascination, on the brown door. Obenreizer, suspiciously observing him, looked that way too.

"There is somebody listening in there! " he exclaimed, with a sharp backward glance at Bintrey.

"There are two people listening, " answered Bintrey.

"Who are they? "

"You shall see. "

With this answer, he raised his voice and spoke the next words—the two common words which are on everybody's lips, at every hour of the day: "Come in! "

The brown door opened. Supported on Marguerite's arm—his sun-burnt colour gone, his right arm bandaged and clung over his breast—Vendale stood before the murderer, a man risen from the dead.

In the moment of silence that followed, the singing of a caged bird in the court-yard outside was the one sound stirring in the room. Maitre Voigt touched Bintrey, and pointed to Obenreizer. "Look at him! " said the notary, in a whisper.

The shock had paralysed every movement in the villain's body, but the movement of the blood. His face was like the face of a corpse. The one vestige of colour left in it was a livid purple streak which marked the course of the scar where his victim had wounded him on the cheek and neck. Speechless, breathless, motionless alike in eye and limb, it seemed as if, at the sight of Vendale, the death to which he had doomed Vendale had struck him where he stood.

"Somebody ought to speak to him, " said Maitre Voigt. "Shall I? "

Even at that moment Bintrey persisted in silencing the notary, and in keeping the lead in the proceedings to himself. Checking Maitre Voigt by a gesture, he dismissed Marguerite and Vendale in these words: —"The object of your appearance here is answered, " he said. "If you will withdraw for the present, it may help Mr. Obenreizer to recover himself. "

It did help him. As the two passed through the door and closed it behind them, he drew a deep breath of relief. He looked round him for the chair from which he had risen, and dropped into it.

"Give him time! " pleaded Maitre Voigt.

"No, " said Bintrey. "I don't know what use he may make of it if I do. " He turned once more to Obenreizer, and went on. "I owe it to myself, " he said—"I don't admit, mind, that I owe it to you—to account for my appearance in these proceedings, and to state what has been done under my advice, and on my sole responsibility. Can you listen to me? "

"I can listen to you. "

"Recall the time when you started for Switzerland with Mr. Vendale, " Bintrey begin. "You had not left England four-and-twenty hours before your niece committed an act of imprudence which not even your penetration could foresee. She followed her promised husband on his journey, without asking anybody's advice or permission, and without any better companion to protect her than a Cellarman in Mr. Vendale's employment. "

"Why did she follow me on the journey? and how came the Cellarman to be the person who accompanied her? "

"She followed you on the journey, " answered Bintrey, "because she suspected there had been some serious collision between you and Mr. Vendale, which had been kept secret from her; and because she rightly believed you to be capable of serving your interests, or of satisfying your enmity, at the price of a crime. As for the Cellarman, he was one, among the other people in Mr. Vendale's establishment, to whom she had applied (the moment your back was turned) to know if anything had happened between their master and you. The Cellarman alone had something to tell her. A senseless superstition, and a common accident which had happened to his master, in his master's cellar, had connected Mr. Vendale in this man's mind with the idea of danger by murder. Your niece surprised him into a confession, which aggravated tenfold the terrors that possessed her. Aroused to a sense of the mischief he had done, the man, of his own accord, made the one atonement in his power. 'If my master is in danger, miss, ' he said, 'it's my duty to follow him, too; and it's more than my duty to take care of *you*. ' The two set forth together—and, for once, a superstition has had its use. It decided your niece on taking the journey; and it led the way to saving a man's life. Do you understand me, so far? "

"I understand you, so far. "

"My first knowledge of the crime that you had committed, " pursued Bintrey, "came to me in the form of a letter from your niece. All you need know is that her love and her courage recovered the body of your victim, and aided the after-efforts which brought him back to life. While he lay helpless at Brieg, under her care, she wrote to me to come out to him. Before starting, I informed Madame Dor that I knew Miss Obenreizer to be safe, and knew where she was. Madame Dor informed me, in return, that a letter had come for your niece, which she knew to be in your handwriting. I took possession of it, and arranged for the forwarding of any other letters which might follow. Arrived at Brieg, I found Mr. Vendale out of danger, and at once devoted myself to hastening the day of reckoning with you. Defresnier and Company turned you off on suspicion; acting on information privately supplied by me. Having stripped you of your false character, the next thing to do was to strip you of your authority over your niece. To reach this end, I not only had no scruple in digging the pitfall under your feet in the dark—I felt a certain professional pleasure in fighting you with your own weapons. By my advice the truth has been carefully concealed from you up to this day. By my advice the trap into which you have walked was set for you (you know why, now, as well as I do) in this place. There was but one certain way of shaking the devilish self-control which has hitherto made you a formidable man. That way has been tried, and (look at me as you may) that way has succeeded. The last thing that remains to be done, " concluded Bintrey, producing two little slips of manuscript from his despatch-box, "is to set your niece free. You have attempted murder, and you have committed forgery and theft. We have the evidence ready against you in both cases. If you are convicted as a felon, you know as well as I do what becomes of your authority over your niece. Personally, I should have preferred taking that way out of it. But considerations are pressed on me which I am not able to resist, and this interview must end, as I have told you already, in a compromise. Sign those lines, resigning all authority over Miss Obenreizer, and pledging yourself never to be seen in England or in Switzerland again; and I will sign an indemnity which secures you against further proceedings on our part. "

Obenreizer took the pen in silence, and signed his niece's release. On receiving the indemnity in return, he rose, but made no movement to leave the room. He stood looking at Maitre Voigt with a strange smile gathering at his lips, and a strange light flashing in his filmy eyes.

"What are you waiting for? " asked Bintrey.

Obenreizer pointed to the brown door. "Call them back, " he answered. "I have something to say in their presence before I go. "

"Say it in my presence, " retorted Bintrey. "I decline to call them back. "

Obenreizer turned to Maitre Voigt. "Do you remember telling me that you once had an English client named Vendale? " he asked.

"Well, " answered the notary. "And what of that? "

"Maitre Voigt, your clock-lock has betrayed you. "

"What do you mean? "

"I have read the letters and certificates in your client's box. I have taken copies of them. I have got the copies here. Is there, or is there not, a reason for calling them back? "

For a moment the notary looked to and fro, between Obenreizer and Bintrey, in helpless astonishment. Recovering himself, he drew his brother-lawyer aside, and hurriedly spoke a few words close at his ear. The face of Bintrey—after first faithfully reflecting the astonishment on the face of Maitre Voigt—suddenly altered its expression. He sprang, with the activity of a young man, to the door of the inner room, entered it, remained inside for a minute, and returned followed by Marguerite and Vendale. "Now, Mr. Obenreizer, " said Bintrey, "the last move in the game is yours. Play it. "

"Before I resign my position as that young lady's guardian, " said Obenreizer, "I have a secret to reveal in which she is interested. In making my disclosure, I am not claiming her attention for a narrative which she, or any other person present, is expected to take on trust. I am possessed of written proofs, copies of originals, the authenticity of which Maitre Voigt himself can attest. Bear that in mind, and permit me to refer you, at starting, to a date long past—the month of February, in the year one thousand eight hundred and thirty-six. "

"Mark the date, Mr. Vendale, " said Bintrey.

"My first proof, " said Obenreizer, taking a paper from his pocket-book. "Copy of a letter, written by an English lady (married) to her sister, a widow. The name of the person writing the letter I shall keep suppressed until I have done. The name of the person to whom the letter is written I am willing to reveal. It is addressed to 'Mrs. Jane Anne Miller, of Groombridge Wells, England. '"

Vendale started, and opened his lips to speak. Bintrey instantly stopped him, as he had stopped Maitre Voigt. "No, " said the pertinacious lawyer. "Leave it to me. "

Obenreizer went on:

"It is needless to trouble you with the first half of the letter, " he said. "I can give the substance of it in two words. The writer's position at the time is this. She has been long living in Switzerland with her husband—obliged to live there for the sake of her husband's health. They are about to move to a new residence on the Lake of Neuchatel in a week, and they will be ready to receive Mrs. Miller as visitor in a fortnight from that time. This said, the writer next enters into an important domestic detail. She has been childless for years—she and her husband have now no hope of children; they are lonely; they want an interest in life; they have decided on adopting a child. Here the important part of the letter begins; and here, therefore, I read it to you word for word. "

He folded back the first page of the letter and read as follows.

"* * * Will you help us, my dear sister, to realise our new project? As English people, we wish to adopt an English child. This may be done, I believe, at the Foundling: my husband's lawyers in London will tell you how. I leave the choice to you, with only these conditions attached to it—that the child is to be an infant under a year old, and is to be a boy. Will you pardon the trouble I am giving you, for my sake; and will you bring our adopted child to us, with your own children, when you come to Neuchatel?

"I must add a word as to my husband's wishes in this matter. He is resolved to spare the child whom we make our own any future mortification and loss of self-respect which might be caused by a discovery of his true origin. He will bear my husband's name, and he will be brought up in the belief that he is really our son. His inheritance of what we have to leave will be secured to him—not only according to the laws of England in such cases, but according to the laws of Switzerland also; for we have lived so long in this country, that there is a doubt whether we may not be considered as I domiciled, in Switzerland. The one precaution left to take is to prevent any after-discovery at the Foundling. Now, our name is a very uncommon one; and if we appear on the Register of the Institution as the persons adopting the child, there is just a chance that something might result from it. Your name, my dear, is the name of thousands of other people; and if you will consent to appear on the Register, there need be no fear of any discoveries in that quarter. We are moving, by the doctor's orders, to a part of Switzerland in which our circumstances are quite unknown; and you, as I understand, are about to engage a new nurse for the journey when you come to see us. Under these circumstances, the child may appear as my child, brought back to me under my sister's care. The only servant we take with us from our old home is my own maid, who can be safely trusted. As for the lawyers in England and in Switzerland, it is their profession to keep secrets—and we may feel quite easy in that direction. So there you have our harmless little conspiracy! Write by return of post, my love, and tell me you will join it. " * * *

"Do you still conceal the name of the writer of that letter? " asked Vendale.

"I keep the name of the writer till the last, " answered Obenreizer, "and I proceed to my second proof—a mere slip of paper this time, as you see. Memorandum given to the Swiss lawyer, who drew the documents referred to in the letter I have just read, expressed as follows: —'Adopted from the Foundling Hospital of England, 3d March, 1836, a male infant, called, in the Institution, Walter Wilding. Person appearing on the register, as adopting the child, Mrs. Jane Anne Miller, widow, acting in this matter for her married sister, domiciled in Switzerland. ' Patience! " resumed Obenreizer, as Vendale, breaking loose from Bintrey, started to his feet. "I shall not keep the name concealed much longer. Two more little slips of paper, and I have done. Third proof! Certificate of Doctor Ganz, still living in practice at Neuchatel, dated July, 1838. The doctor certifies (you shall read it for yourselves directly), first, that he attended the adopted child in its infant maladies; second, that, three months before the date of the certificate, the gentleman adopting the child as his son died; third, that on the date of the certificate, his widow and her maid, taking the adopted child with them, left Neuchatel on their return to England. One more link now added to this, and my chain of evidence is complete. The maid remained with her mistress till her mistress's death, only a few years since. The maid can swear to the identity of the adopted infant, from his childhood to his youth—from his youth to his manhood, as he is now. There is her address in England—and there, Mr. Vendale, is the fourth, and final proof! "

"Why do you address yourself to *me*? " said Vendale, as Obenreizer threw the written address on the table.

Obenreizer turned on him, in a sudden frenzy of triumph.

"*Because you are the man*! If my niece marries you, she marries a bastard, brought up by public charity. If my niece marries you, she marries an impostor, without name or lineage, disguised in the character of a gentleman of rank and family. "

"Bravo! " cried Bintrey. "Admirably put, Mr. Obenreizer! It only wants one word more to complete it. She marries—thanks entirely to your exertions—a man who inherits a handsome fortune, and a man whose origin will make him prouder than ever of his peasant-wife. George Vendale, as brother-executors, let us congratulate each other! Our dear dead friend's last wish on earth is accomplished. We have found the lost Walter Wilding. As Mr. Obenreizer said just now— you are the man! "

The words passed by Vendale unheeded. For the moment he was conscious of but one sensation; he heard but one voice. Marguerite's hand was clasping his. Marguerite's voice was whispering to him:

"I never loved you, George, as I love you now! "

## THE CURTAIN FALLS

May-day. There is merry-making in Cripple Corner, the chimneys smoke, the patriarchal dining-hall is hung with garlands, and Mrs. Goldstraw, the respected housekeeper, is very busy. For, on this bright morning the young master of Cripple Corner is married to its young mistress, far away: to wit, in the little town of Brieg, in

Switzerland, lying at the foot of the Simplon Pass where she saved his life.

The bells ring gaily in the little town of Brieg, and flags are stretched across the street, and rifle shots are heard, and sounding music from brass instruments. Streamer-decorated casks of wine have been rolled out under a gay awning in the public way before the Inn, and there will be free feasting and revelry. What with bells and banners, draperies hanging from windows, explosion of gunpowder, and reverberation of brass music, the little town of Brieg is all in a flutter, like the hearts of its simple people.

It was a stormy night last night, and the mountains are covered with snow. But the sun is bright to-day, the sweet air is fresh, the tin spires of the little town of Brieg are burnished silver, and the Alps are ranges of far-off white cloud in a deep blue sky.

The primitive people of the little town of Brieg have built a greenwood arch across the street, under which the newly married pair shall pass in triumph from the church. It is inscribed, on that side, "HONOUR AND LOVE TO MARGUERITE VENDALE! " for the people are proud of her to enthusiasm. This greeting of the bride under her new name is affectionately meant as a surprise, and therefore the arrangement has been made that she, unconscious why, shall be taken to the church by a tortuous back way. A scheme not difficult to carry into execution in the crooked little town of Brieg.

So, all things are in readiness, and they are to go and come on foot. Assembled in the Inn's best chamber, festively adorned, are the bride and bridegroom, the Neuchatel notary, the London lawyer, Madame Dor, and a certain large mysterious Englishman, popularly known as Monsieur Zhoe- Ladelle. And behold Madame Dor, arrayed in a spotless pair of gloves of her own, with no hand in the air, but both hands clasped round the neck of the bride; to embrace whom Madame Dor has turned her broad back on the company, consistent to the last.

"Forgive me, my beautiful, " pleads Madame Dor, "for that I ever was his she-cat! "

"She-cat, Madame Dor?

"Engaged to sit watching my so charming mouse, " are the explanatory words of Madame Dor, delivered with a penitential sob.

"Why, you were our best friend! George, dearest, tell Madame Dor. Was she not our best friend? "

"Undoubtedly, darling. What should we have done without her? "

"You are both so generous, " cries Madame Dor, accepting consolation, and immediately relapsing. "But I commenced as a she-cat. "

"Ah! But like the cat in the fairy-story, good Madame Dor, " says Vendale, saluting her cheek, "you were a true woman. And, being a true woman, the sympathy of your heart was with true love. "

"I don't wish to deprive Madame Dor of her share in the embraces that are going on, " Mr. Bintrey puts in, watch in hand, "and I don't presume to offer any objection to your having got yourselves mixed together, in the corner there, like the three Graces. I merely remark that I think it's time we were moving. What are *your* sentiments on that subject, Mr. Ladle? "

"Clear, sir, " replies Joey, with a gracious grin. "I'm clearer altogether, sir, for having lived so many weeks upon the surface. I never was half so long upon the surface afore, and it's done me a power of good. At Cripple Corner, I was too much below it. Atop of the Simpleton, I was a deal too high above it. I've found the medium here, sir. And if ever I take it in convivial, in all the rest of my days, I mean to do it this day, to the toast of 'Bless 'em both. '"

"I, too! " says Bintrey. "And now, Monsieur Voigt, let you and me be two men of Marseilles, and allons, marchons, arm-in-arm! "

They go down to the door, where others are waiting for them, and they go quietly to the church, and the happy marriage takes place. While the ceremony is yet in progress, the notary is called out. When it is finished, he has returned, is standing behind Vendale, and touches him on the shoulder.

"Go to the side door, one moment, Monsieur Vendale. Alone. Leave Madame to me. "

At the side door of the church, are the same two men from the Hospice. They are snow-stained and travel-worn. They wish him joy, and then each lays his broad hand upon Vendale's breast, and one says in a low voice, while the other steadfastly regards him:

"It is here, Monsieur. Your litter. The very same. "

"My litter is here? Why? "

"Hush! For the sake of Madame. Your companion of that day —"

"What of him? "

The man looks at his comrade, and his comrade takes him up. Each keeps his hand laid earnestly on Vendale's breast.

"He had been living at the first Refuge, monsieur, for some days. The weather was now good, now bad. "

"Yes? "

"He arrived at our Hospice the day before yesterday, and, having refreshed himself with sleep on the floor before the fire, wrapped in his cloak, was resolute to go on, before dark, to the next Hospice. He had a great fear of that part of the way, and thought it would be worse to-morrow. "

"Yes? "

"He went on alone. He had passed the gallery when an avalanche — like that which fell behind you near the Bridge of the Ganther —"

"Killed him? "

"We dug him out, suffocated and broken all to pieces! But, monsieur, as to Madame. We have brought him here on the litter, to be buried. We must ascend the street outside. Madame must not see. It would be an accursed thing to bring the litter through the arch across the street, until Madame has passed through. As you descend, we who accompany the litter will set it down on the stones of the street the second to the right, and will stand before it. But do not let Madame turn her head towards the street the second to the right. There is no time to lose. Madame will be alarmed by your absence. Adieu! "

Vendale returns to his bride, and draws her hand through his unmainied arm. A pretty procession awaits them at the main door of the church. They take their station in it, and descend the street amidst the ringing of the bells, the firing of the guns, the waving of the flags, the playing of the music, the shouts, the smiles, and tears, of the excited town. Heads are uncovered as she passes, hands are kissed to her, all the people bless her. "Heaven's benediction on the dear girl! See where she goes in her youth and beauty; she who so nobly saved his life! "

Near the corner of the street the second to the right, he speaks to her, and calls her attention to the windows on the opposite side. The corner well passed, he says: "Do not look round, my darling, for a reason that I have, " and turns his head. Then, looking back along the street, he sees the litter and its bearers passing up alone under the arch, as he and she and their marriage train go down towards the shining valley.

Lightning Source UK Ltd.
Milton Keynes UK
UKHW010849100921
390347UK00001B/171